crush. candy. corpse.

crush. candy. corpse.

sylvia mcnicoll

LORIMER

James Lorimer & Company Ltd., Publishers
Toronto

James Lorimer & Company Ltd., Publishers acknowledges the support of the Ontario Arts Council. We acknowledge the financial support of the Government of Canada through the Canada Book Fund for our publishing activities. We acknowledge the support of the Canada Council for the Arts which last year invested $24.3 million in writing and publishing throughout Canada. We acknowledge the Government of Ontario through the Ontario Media Development Corporation's Ontario Book Initiative.

   Canada

Library and Archives Canada Cataloguing in Publication

McNicoll, Sylvia, 1954-
    Crush candy corpse / Sylvia McNicoll.

Issued also in electronic formats.
ISBN 978-1-4594-0063-4 (bound).--ISBN 978-1-4594-0062-7 (pbk.)

    I. Title.

PS8575.N52C78 2012   jC813'.54   C2012-900032-9

James Lorimer & Company Ltd., Publishers
317 Adelaide Street West, Suite 1002
Toronto, ON, Canada
M5V 1P9
www.lorimer.ca

Distributed in the United States by:
Orca Book Publishers
P.O. Box 468
Custer, WA USA
98240-0468

Printed and bound in Canada.

Manufactured by Friesens in Altona, Manitoba, Canada in September 2012.
Job #79096

For Mom.
First she forgot how to walk, then how to
chew and swallow, and finally how to breathe.
We will always remember her.

Disappointment of the family, not at all like my older brother Wolfgang who is minding the office so Mom and Dad can be here. Next to Mom sits Dad, slightly shorter but square shouldered and strong. He and Wolfgang look alike — guys you can instantly trust and lean on.

My family is the only reason I'm considering this dragged-out process and I know they'll stand behind me no matter what. Still, what happens if I'm found guilty? The sentence will be way worse — a couple of years in a youth correctional centre, at least.

Twelve jury members stare vacantly at me from the left side of the courtroom, waiting for my answer. They're going to decide my fate. Really?

My lawyer told me to dress in smart-casual, but I'm guessing no one instructed the jury. The best-dressed one wears a kiwi-coloured sweatsuit, the worst wears relaxed-fit jeans and a long-sleeved, red plaid shirt. Then there's the lady in the front with a stained top, a fat guy wearing a polo shirt with horizontal stripes, and a guy with broken horn-rimmed glasses that make his head look tilted in a question. Two young guys with identical goatees fidget at the back. One has multiple piercings and looks as though the rings in his eyebrows and lips are the only things holding him together. The other scratches his beard a lot. Five more jurors look like they've just left the bowling alley or their jobs as greeters in a big-box store.

That jury doesn't know that I took a half an hour to press my clothes. Maybe that's good. Maybe they'd hold it against me — excessive neatness, sign of a serial killer in the making. I'm wearing a dark grey skirt, a pale rose shirt, and low-heeled pumps. A subdued look except for the pink streaks in my hair.

The guy in the glasses yawns, checks his watch, then

chapter one

"Sonja Anna Ehret, you stand accused of manslaughter. How do you plead?"

It's been a year since it happened and now, here I stand, front row centre in a courtroom. Four windowless, beige walls surround me, and I find it hard to breathe, let alone answer. Silence hangs heavy and musty.

A couple of clerks watch me from behind a long desk. Dressed in black robes, they're like crows on a wire between me and an eagle, the judge. He trains his eyes on me from a higher perch, a throne-like desk flanked on either side by a flag.

The clock on the wall ticks slowly forward. Everyone's waiting for my answer.

A man with a clipboard sits on the opposite side of the room. A reporter. Why doesn't he sit on my side?

I want to plead guilty. Immediately the trial would end and the sentence would be lighter — probation and a few hundred hours of community service. But it would kill my parents, especially Mom.

She sits behind me, tall, pale, and thin, with her chin held high. She's a proud woman and I'm already the Big glances over at me. Still waiting.

"Sunny?" Michael McCann, my lawyer, prompts. I look down to the right where he stands. Another crow in a black robe. Or maybe a raven. His hair is dark and closely cropped, and everything about him seems sharper than those clerks at the front. His brown eyes measure me.

Guilty, guilty, guilty. My heart flip-flops. This is it; I'm going to say it. Who cares what the lawyer told me to say? Can he honestly believe this jury will acquit me?

I face the unsmiling bald judge. He's wearing a jaunty red sash across his robe. I focus on that diagonal slash of red. *Guilty,* I say in my mind and tell my mouth to follow. But for some reason, that stripe of colour gives me hope. Instead, I speak out as clearly as I can.

"Not guilty."

The judge raises his eyebrows at me. *Oh really?* "Very well," he says out loud. "Mr. Dougal, are you prepared to make the opening statement?"

The Crown prosecutor nods and approaches his stand like a large vulture, his robe floating behind him. His skin and hair look white against the blackness of the robe, his eyes are window-cleaner blue. "Your Honour, members of the jury . . ." he stares their way till all of them pay attention, "we will prove that on February 14, 2011, the defendant entered the Paradise Manor Longterm Care residence and willfully fed hard candy to Helen Demers, a known diabetic who also had difficulty swallowing due to her Alzheimer's." The jurors squirm under his stare and he swivels to focus on me instead. He looks towards the judge now. "Evidence will show Sonja had a relationship with Cole, the victim's grandson, and that she carried out his pact with his grandmother to assist her in suicide.

We will show that when the victim began to asphyxiate, the defendant walked away, purposely failing to provide medical assistance."

My mother coughs but it's really the cover-up for a sob. I turn slightly and see her head bowed, her shoulders shaking. Dad slips his arm around her.

Beside her, my lawyer nods his head as though all of this was part of his plan, but his eyes go all teddy-bear soft whenever Mom cries.

The Crown prosecutor approaches my seat. "With the consent of Defence, we have entered the coroner's report to show the details of this death." He pauses and looks at me hard again, a vulture after a rabbit. "I now call my first witness, Adam Brooks, to the stand. Adam Brooks, do you wish to take the oath on the Bible or —"

"The Bible." Mr. Brooks swears in and tells the court how he was my Grade 11 English and homeroom teacher last year when all this happened. He wears a dark jacket, light shirt, and a cherry-coloured tie. His hair lies combed and flat against his head. He's made a big effort for me and I appreciate it.

"How would you characterize Sonja Ehret as a student?"

Mr. Brooks digs his forefinger between his tie and his neck. Behind those silver-rimmed, round glasses, his eyes look trapped. I know he wants to say nice things, but he's also a stickler about the truth. "Average."

My father clears his throat behind me.

The thing is, I handed in my homework on time and it was always neatly printed out in 14-point Times New Roman, as he liked it. I just didn't sweat over the content as much as he wanted. The other thing is, I sat at the back where my best friend Alexis and me passed notes and chatted from time to time, and that ticked him off.

"Would you say she is a truthful person?"

"Objection." My lawyer jumps to his feet and gestures to the prosecutor. "Your Honour, my friend is asking Mr. Brooks to form an opinion."

"Sustained."

The vulture does a quick eye roll, one I'm sure he doesn't want the judge to see. "Can I direct the court to exhibit A, on the screen? Mr. Brooks, would you kindly explain to the court what this is?"

"Sure. I always try to get the students to write about their own experiences. They were asked to journal about their volunteer work. On the screen is the first entry from Sonja's volunteer log."

Imagine, to graduate we have to perform forty hours of volunteer work in the community. Forty hours at Paradise Manor. A sentence in itself. But Mr. Brooks gave me a second sentence: I had to document and respond to what happened to me along the way.

The First Visit — thirty-eight hours left

The sewer exploded! Honestly! Today was supposed to be my volunteer training at Paradise Manor, but because my ride cancelled out on me and the bus driver needed to detour around a broken pipe on Harvester, I arrived at the seniors' home late. I waited at the front desk for at least fifteen minutes, but Mrs. Johnson never came and I couldn't see a book to sign in. There was no one around to ask. I would have looked for her but a terrible odour filled the foyer — methane gas, I was sure of it. I figured that another pipe must have burst and Mrs. Johnson was busy evacuating the residents, because judging by the level of stink, the home was about to blow. A nurse came into the foyer, and I asked her about the methane leak and how long we had till the whole place went up. She just stared at me, but that did happen in that Mexican resort, Mr. Brooks, so I told her I needed some air and left. But I showed up for my volunteer work, Mr. Brooks, and waited and waited, so I think this should count towards my forty hours.

Okay, Paradise Manor smelled so bad I wanted to hurl, but truthfully, I didn't think a pipe would explode. All I knew was that I couldn't take it, so when Donovan (my boyfriend at the time) finally texted me that he could pick me up, I dashed outside to make my escape into the fresh air.

I guess the nurse must have told Mrs. Johnson about my methane leak comment, and of course she took it personally. That really started our relationship on a bad note.

She never could find it in her to change her mind about me, which is why she insisted the police charge me with manslaughter.

I wish I could explain all this to the jury, but I won't get a chance to talk until the end. What I want to say is this: The definition of the word volunteer, straight from the dictionary, is "to perform a service of one's own free will." But there's no free will involved if you have to do it in order to graduate. Forty hours! Our principal suggested we do it this year so that it wouldn't interfere with our heavier course load and part-time jobs in our final one. He thought our volunteer work might "inform" our work choices. Mr. Brooks forced the issue by assigning us that volunteer journal.

It's not like Paradise Manor was my choice. I wanted to put in my forty hours at Salon Teo — where I'm still hoping to get an apprenticeship — but Mr. Brooks said no. I had to work for a charitable cause. My friends Lee, Christopher, Liam, and Sasha snagged placements at our local cable station. While that television channel deserves everyone's sympathy, I can't see how it qualifies as a charity. Mr. Brooks said because they video City Hall meetings and local events like the Santa Claus Parade and the Art Auction — they serve the community.

I could have swept up the hair of the mayor's wife or shampooed and rinsed out the dye from the Culture Centre chairman's hair. I give the best scalp massages when I shampoo. I could have helped them look great for the camera and maybe if they would have felt good, the mayor and the council might have approved the budget for the extension on the museum. People underestimate these things, but just look around at the state of the world and the way people's grooming and dressing habits have gone. You can't deny that the two are linked.

But appearance has never been important to Mr. Brooks. He wears saggy-bottomed jeans and faded golf shirts and runs his fingers through his long, grey hair as though they're a substitute for a quality ion-free ceramic hairbrush.

The choices for placements were running out. My boyfriend had held out till his final year to volunteer. He chose helping at the food bank 'cause it was the closest thing to working out in a gym that he could find. Donovan, dark and good-looking — my parents had forbidden me to see him after we got caught shoplifting together. But I just couldn't quit him then.

Alexis took me to sign up with her for the animal shelter,

but there was only one spot left and I let her have it. I wasn't being a hero — that place reeked of antiseptic and dog doo, and I have a sensitive nose.

One of the other girls in my class, Lena, was trained at clown school — no, really — and hung out with terminally ill kids at the hospital, which I found depressing.

After school, once I had finally been forced into the last placement, I tried to explain my "choice" to Donovan.

"But Sunny, old people are even more depressing 'cause they are definitely going to die." He caught my hand and held it as we walked out of school together.

"You're right." I squeezed his palm with my fingers as we went down the walkway and into the parking lot towards his car. "My grandmother died when I was six," I told him as he opened the door for me. "Still, I think she was the person who liked me best in all the world."

Donovan swung me around and looked into my eyes. "I like you a lot."

I couldn't help smiling. "I guess."

He gently pushed back the pink strands of hair framing my face and kissed me.

Like, not love, I thought as we broke apart.

chapter two

The prosecuting buzzard tips his beak expectantly. "Mr. Brooks, for this volunteer project, what did Mrs. Johnson, Paradise Manor's supervisor, tell you about Sonja's duties and how her attendance would be monitored?"

Looking uneasy, Mr. Brooks folds his fingers on the desk. "Mrs. Johnson insisted on Sonja signing in and out." He frowns then and opens his fingers again as though he needs their help. "Sonja would assist with feedings and various recreational activities for the residents."

"From your statement, I understand that after Sonja failed to show up for volunteer training the first day, you called Mrs. Johnson and asked her what happened." The buzzard cups his hand around his chin. "Could you tell the court what you found out?" He sounds genuinely interested, as if he hasn't pored over the notes and heard the story a hundred times already.

Mr. Brooks nods sadly. "Mrs. Johnson said that she hadn't seen Sonja and that she hadn't signed in. When I asked her whether there had been a sewer problem, she became defensive. She said the residents may have had digestive issues but her staff did their best to clean them up quickly.

There just weren't enough hands. She said that Sonja would see that if she ever came back."

"Your Honour, I would like to point out that while Mr. Brooks's testimony is largely hearsay, it is entered with consent, as Mrs. Johnson will be testifying later in the trial." The buzzard flips through his notes. The clock on the wall seems to stop entirely.

The lady in the kiwi-coloured sweatsuit closes her eyes. As long as she sleeps only during the Crown's time, I should be fine.

The buzzard looks up at Mr. Brooks. "In order for Sonja to return to Paradise Manor, what conditions did she have to fulfill?"

Mr. Brooks glances my way, but it's as though he sees through me. "Mrs. Johnson and I agreed that she could attend a St. John Ambulance course to make up for some of the volunteer training she missed at the residence. The rest she could pick up on the job."

The prosecutor speaks louder. "And what did she learn at the course?"

The lady in the sweats wakes up again.

"As I understand it from the St. John Ambulance outline, basic first aid."

"Could I direct the court's attention to exhibit A again, the next entry?

The Second Visit — thirty-six hours left
Mr. Brooks, I went to the all-day St. John Ambulance course to learn emergency first aid like you and Mrs. Johnson said I had to. The instructor taught us how to tend to cuts, bleeding, and broken limbs. Also how to

perform abdominal thrusts and CPR on a big, grey plastic dummy.

Then I went to Paradise Manor after school on Monday. It seems they fixed their plumbing problems because it didn't smell so bad. Lucky because it was dinner time. I was assigned to help feed Johann Schwartz, which was difficult because he talked a lot — in German. He choked all the time and he looked frail. I wondered whether jabbing the heel of my hand under his ribs to perform the Heimlich wouldn't crush a bone or two. I mean, I'm glad I learned all that first aid and I'll use it at Salon Teo if any of the clients ever have a heart attack or choke on a stick of gum or something. But here at the residence, I'll call a nurse.

What's he getting at by showing that entry? Is he trying to convince the jury that I never intended to use first aid to help any of the seniors? Does the jury realize how hard you have to jab into a person to perform the Heimlich? They should all go see for themselves how fragile the residents are.

As for the odour, Alexis had a method for conquering smell that she used when she volunteered at the animal shelter. I decided to test it. I put some Vicks VapoRub up my nose and called Donovan. He agreed to a walk at Sulphur Springs, where the water smells like boiled eggs.

"If you have a cold, we could have gone another time," he complained when I got in the car.

I explained my experiment.

"Oh Sunny, no. You can't block up stink with more stink. Let's go to the perfume department at The Bay. I'll get you a nice musk and that will be way more pleasant for everyone around you."

When he says "get," I'm never sure he means "buy." But I didn't want to insult him, so I let him drive me to the mall. First I washed off the Vicks in the ladies' room, then we headed for the cosmetic department where I sampled a number of scents. "Donovan, what about this one?" I asked after a third lady in a white jacket sprayed my wrist. Why was Donovan so far away? "Donovan?"

From the third counter over, he shook his head at me and winked.

Oh no. I stepped away from the woman all ready to spray me with Excitement, the latest cologne out for the fall. "Um, that's all right. I can't smell the difference anymore."

"Here." She offered me a coffee bean. "Wave it under your nose. It will cleanse the palate."

I did and the little brown bean actually overpowered all the sweet flowery smells. Wow. Right then and there I realized the solution to my problem with Paradise Manor. No purchase or theft required. "Um, thank you." I waved madly at Donovan, then smiled at the cosmetics clerk. "We'll come back another day."

Still, back in the car, Donovan proudly presented me with an Eau de la Terre tester. "Sorry. Couldn't get you an unopened bottle."

"Donovan!" I pulled my hands away.

"What? It's a green perfume, made from organic ingredients. Never tested on animals."

"I can't get picked up for shoplifting again. Next time it will stay on my record."

"If I thought I would get caught, I wouldn't have grabbed it." He pushed the cologne to me.

I shook my head at him.

"Oh, come on. It's not a small store." He sprayed some in the air and it did smell nice. "No one's gonna take a hit for it. They've got insurance." Donovan smiled then, and his dimples melted my heart. "You know I would have bought it for you if I'd had any money."

I frowned. But I couldn't stay mad at him for long. He'd stolen for me, after all. Finally I took the cologne and sprayed some on my wrist.

Then Donovan kissed me.

The next day Wolfie helped Alexis and me make coffee-bean necklaces. We found we couldn't poke the needle through, so he stuck the beans in some putty and drilled the holes for us first. I had a green sweater the beads would really offset nicely. Maybe I'd wear my earth-toned gypsy skirt, too. Theme-wise it would go well with the Terre cologne.

Monday after school I waited for Mrs. Johnson in the lobby of Paradise Manor. It was very cozy there. A gas fireplace burned cheerily and a few life-sized ceramic dogs sprawled across an oriental rug. Then a poufy-haired woman in a skirt and jacket set bustled in. All business, that was Mrs. Johnson. She made me fill out some forms as we sat on the leather easy chairs in front of that fire. Then she insisted I head for the counter to sign the guestbook and use the hand sanitizer. That stuff smells like insect repellent and vinegar combined. You can actually use it as a lice killer — I read that in a magazine. I took a quick whiff of my necklace and ran my hands over the beads to get rid of the scent.

Next she introduced me to Gillian Halliday, the volunteer coordinator, who had a wide, white grin and a head full of tiny braids.

"It's time for the patients' supper," Gillian told me. "Let's head for the dining room and you can help me feed Johann." She keyed in four numbers to open the door. "The code is 7686, but if you forget, it's written at the bottom of the box underneath this lid." I peeked in and, sure enough, saw the numbers on a white paper. As Gillian pushed the door shut behind us, the cozy feeling left. The door itself was camouflaged with a mural of a bookshelf. "Be careful comin' in so you don't let any of the old folks out," Gillian told me.

"They want to escape?" She didn't have to answer. The walls were beige and blank; the floor was speckled linoleum. Windows opened to a nursing station to the right. It was an airless atmosphere. Who wouldn't want to get out?

A sweet old couple strolled hand in hand towards us.

"Hello, Fred. Hi, Marlene," Gillian called in a jolly voice. "Almost time to eat. Don't walk too far!"

Fred shuffled along with one grey sweatpant leg tucked into a sock. So goofy looking — I wanted to run and pull it out. Why didn't one of the aides do that?

"I don't understand it," he grumbled as he tried the hidden door. "They must have changed something."

Marlene kept her head down, murmuring back at him. I could only see her forehead. On it was a lump the size of a dinosaur egg. "Should we stop in and pick up some bread?" she asked Fred.

He murmured back, "Can't stop now."

"Do they understand each other?" I asked Gillian.

She shrugged her shoulders and then grabbed Fred's arm. "This way," she said, as she gently turned the couple around.

We followed behind them. Dressed in pastel polyester — baby blue pants covered by a pink floral scoop top — Marlene's colours actually worked for her. Still, her hair was an iron grey, and there's so much a good colour rinse can do for that. "Nice that they can stay together anyway," I told Gillian, getting more depressed by the minute.

"Oh, they're not married to each other. The Alzheimer's makes them want to pace. So one day they just started strolling together, holding hands. I have to stop them sometimes. Fred once collapsed from all the walking."

"Really. What happened to Marlene's head?"

"The old folks lose their sense of balance as they get on. She fell out of bed."

"Ouch!" But it wasn't the big lump that made me squirm, it was the way her neck jutted out, like a turkey stretching to get a worm, head down. I pulled back my shoulders and rubbed at the top of my spine. Would my neck look like that someday?

"Here we are, the dining room."

I could see it through windows in the hall — blue walls with murals of '50s-type teens, blue cloths draped over wooden tables, a cafeteria-style counter where trays of food were lined up, ready to go. Prettied-up institutional. Imagine eating every meal of your life in there.

Outside the door six wheelchairs circled the area, the residents in them paused in semi-doze mode.

"Hello, Gorgeous. What a lovely dress you have on!"

I turned to see a smiling, silver-haired lady with lively dark eyes and bright red lips. Lipstick? How civilized. She was sitting in a chair behind a walker. Was she talking to me? I was wearing a skirt, not a dress.

"Jeannette, this is Sunny, our new volunteer." Gillian winked at me.

Jeannette continued to look at me, so I assumed it had been my clothing that she complimented. "Thank you," I answered and smiled back at her. Perhaps there was one person not so far gone here. I mean, she mixed up her words but she still had taste.

Jeannette grinned, teeth showing now and just a touch of that red lipstick on her incisor. "You're welcome." Her head turned slightly, attention somewhere else. Suddenly her lips pulled down into a vicious dog snarl.

"If you touch my walker again, I will kill you."

Whoa! I stepped back. Did she have a hidden weapon? Who was she even mad at? The lady she seemed to be threatening slumped in her chair, mouth open as she lightly snored. Could she have moved in her sleep?

"You should make her stop!" Jeannette snapped at Gillian. "Take her to her room or tie her hands to the chair."

"You know I'm not going to do that." Gillian frowned at her and then abruptly changed the subject. "Have you seen the dinners you have to choose from tonight?" She gestured at a menu posted on the dining-room window.

Jeannette shuffled to her feet. Was Gillian trying to distract her? Seemed to be working, anyway. She wheeled her walker closer to the door. The menu showed a choice of two meals: schnitzel or meatloaf. That sounded pretty good. At least if the seniors had to eat in a cafeteria the rest of their lives, it was nice that they could still choose their meals.

Gillian faced me. "We have a Hungarian chef and he's terrific. If you could take charge of Johann over there and get as much food into him as you can before he falls asleep, that would be wonderful."

I walked over to the man she had pointed to. He looked

22

pretty skinny. His head slumped onto his hand. While he had a very high forehead, the hair he had left was jet black with silver wings at the side. A Dracula look. I liked it.

"Just kick off the brakes and wheel him up to the middle table. I'll hold the door for you," Gillian instructed me.

As I pushed the chair forward, Johann snapped up. "*Was ist loss?*"

"He only speaks German."

"*Was ist loss?*" he repeated more loudly.

My own grandma spoke German and I replied with some words I remembered her saying to me. "*Ich liebe dich.*"

His face softened and he relaxed back into his chair. "*Schatzie, ich liebe dich auch.*"

"Yeah, yeah. You love everybody, Johann." Gillian chuckled. "You're just a big playboy."

My face flushed as the meaning of the words came back to me. Omi had hugged me and told me she loved me in German. And I had just told Johann.

Gillian grinned broadly at me. "Honey, you're a natural. You'll have him eatin' out of the palm of your hand."

After I parked him at his spot by the table, I covered my cheeks with my hands to stop blushing.

"You're doing great, Sunny. Keep up the good work."

It was an insane asylum, but I was doing great. It figured.

"Put the bib around his neck."

The bib looked like a large pot holder. I laid it underneath Johann's chin, fastening the Velcro at the back. Then a dining-room attendant set a tray down in front of Johann. "There you go, Papa."

I lifted the beige plastic lid covering his plate. "What is this?" I asked. The matching plate divided his meal into three sections: a plop of white mush, a plop of red, and a plop of brown.

"You read the menu, it's schnitzel, ground up so he can swallow it." The dining-room attendant set another tray in front of Fred, sitting right across from us now.

I never heard her ask for his menu selection. When Fred lifted his lid, I could recognize the meatloaf, peas, and potatoes.

I stared at the attendant, a tiny woman with hair way too dark for her pale complexion. Accidental goth. I know she would be happier if I could tone down that black to a chestnut and maybe add some highlights. And if she were happier, maybe Fred could have had his choice of suppers.

Suddenly, something clattered to the floor and I looked towards the noise. A red bicycle helmet spun across the room. A tall kid who looked about my age chased after it. That helmet probably accounted for his stick-up blond hair. Once he scooped it up, he joined a lady at another table.

"Meatloaf, Grandma. Your favourite!" he said to her as the cafeteria goth set down another tray. He beamed at her as he helped her spoon some of her supper up. What fun he seemed to be having.

How come I wasn't having any? I frowned as I concentrated on feeding Johann. One way or the other I was going to get through my forty hours. Despite the craziness surrounding me, I would get this meal into Johann and show everyone how well I could do at this placement. One spoonful, then another, then another. I was going to get it in him and write about it for my A in English. He clenched his mouth shut now. "Come on." I nudged his lips with a spoon. Were his eyes drooping? He couldn't fall asleep on me yet. He'd hardly eaten anything on his plate.

"*Ich liebe dich,*" I called out in desperation. I didn't even care that he wasn't my type.

His eyes and mouth popped open and I shoved another mouthful into him.

"Isn't he a little old for you?" the scrawny kid called. "Do you want my phone number, instead?"

"As if!" I rolled my eyes. "Have some apple juice, Johann." I tipped the glass and some trickled down the sides of his mouth.

Hek, hek, hek. He began coughing. From my St. John Ambulance course I knew he was fine. As long as his colour remained normal and he could make a noise, he could breathe. I gave him another sip but it didn't help. *Hek, hek, hek.*

From out of nowhere the supervisor, Mrs. Johnson, rushed at me. "Slower, slower! Can't you see the poor man is choking!"

I pulled the cup away. She wasn't exactly yelling, but definitely scolding with a stiff tone, kind of the way my mother talked to me sometimes. My cheeks burned. Too bad, for a moment there I'd been brilliant.

chapter three

"Does the defence have any questions for Mr. Brooks?"

My lawyer, Michael McCann, stands up, straightening his robe behind him. "Thank you, Your Honour, yes," he says to the judge and then turns to the witness stand. "Mr. Brooks, from your classroom discussions and Sonja's volunteer journal, can you explain how the position was working out for her?"

Mr. Brooks nods. "At first, I didn't think she'd go back because of the odour issues. I knew she was sensitive to smells when after the second class she'd asked me privately to switch seats because of a student's perspiration problem." Mr. Brooks struggles for a second. "I thought the seniors in that part of the residence might prove too upsetting for her. But I was pleasantly surprised. Not only did she return, but I got the impression that she was almost enjoying her placement."

My lawyer looks down at his binder of notes, flipping a page over. "And back to that first volunteer journal entry, how do you explain why she returned if she didn't truly believe that the odour was a temporary problem?"

Mr. Brooks pulls at the knot of his tie again with one finger and frowns. "I don't know. I just thought she reached for something bigger inside herself and forced herself to overcome her aversion. It's what we hope for when we assign students volunteer work — that they become better people."

My lawyer turns to the jury and repeats in a louder voice, "Becoming better people . . . No further questions." He sits down again.

A few of them nod and the lady in the front smiles. He's scored some points for me, I can tell.

The buzzard rises. "The Crown calls to the stand Katherine Filmore."

Now what can she possibly know about the events of that day? And it has to be bad stuff or the Crown wouldn't use her as a witness.

Katherine walks up to the witness box and gets sworn in. Occupation? "Receptionist," she tells everyone. She's medium old and usually wears half glasses when she mans the front desk at Paradise Manor. Today she's specless and sports a bright silk scarf around her neck.

I barely talked to the lady — except when she was reminding me about the rules, which I tried to follow most of the time. Why don't they check the rest of my journal entries instead of talking to her? They have them all. They would learn more about me that way.

The Third Visit — thirty-four hours left

Next visit I arrived early, signed in, and washed my hands. Then I used the code to open the lockup unit and walked in by myself. I smiled and said hello to all the seniors I met. I chatted with a few, helped some with basic grooming, and, as usual, took Mr. Schwartz into the dining room where we celebrated Fred, Jeannette, Susan, and Helen's birthdays.

Donovan couldn't drive me that day. At lunch he told me he had detention, so I texted my brother who answered, *Busy. Use bus. xoxoxo.* Drat, he was the one person I could always rely on. Now how was I supposed to get to Paradise Manor on time? Honestly.

Then, just before last period, Donovan caught me at my locker and asked if I wanted to shop for my prom dress.

"No, Donny. I've got my volunteer work today. Remember?"

He put his arm around my waist. "Cut it short and I'll come get you. We can spend a couple hours together."

"Not today." I shrugged away. "I have to be at Mom's office by seven tonight or she'll figure out I'm still seeing you."

Donovan squinted at me and frowned. Suddenly, he smiled at someone walking behind me. I turned to see. Summer. A senior (not the grey-haired kind) with long hair and legs. She smiled back.

How could she not? Donovan's eyes are this smoky brown . . .

I elbowed him. "Tomorrow or the next day we can go shopping. We just can't hang together after school today."

He caught my chin in his hand. "You don't have to do your volunteer work this year just because Brooks is forcing you to journal."

I hesitated half a second, distracted by his fingers touching my neck. "Yeah, I do. And I have to do well, too, not like Some People." I pulled away. It was always so hard to do the right thing around Donovan. I found myself explaining. "Mom said I could work at Salon Teo next year if my grades were good." Dream eyes or not, he couldn't wreck this for me. He caught my arms and pulled me close. Then he kissed me, long and slow so I couldn't breathe for a moment. That made me late for class, but it still didn't change my mind.

Last period I had Mr. Brooks, so I asked if I could leave before the bell to get the 3:20 bus and he let me. I wasn't looking forward to working around Mrs. Johnson — clearly she didn't like me — but as I arrived at Paradise Manor that tall kid rode up on his bicycle, which was red like his helmet. The brightness of the colour perked me up and I waved at him.

He took off his helmet. His hair was standing up, kind of like a rooster's comb. "Hi there. I'm Cole . . . Cole Demers, Helen's grandson. You're that new volunteer." He grinned as he held out the hand with the helmet in it. I wasn't sure if I was supposed to shake it. "The one who's in love with Johann."

"Yeah, yeah. Whatever." I shook my head. "I'm Sonja Ehret. My friends call me Sunny." I looked into his eyes, which were the nicest thing about him. They were a golden caramel colour and they seemed friendly.

"Could you just hold onto that while I lock up my bike?"

"Sure." My fingers itched to pat down his hair. "Um, do you want to borrow some product?" I asked when he straightened and began walking with me.

"Excuse me?"

"For your hair. I have some Smooth in my purse."

"Smooth?"

"You know, it's that new hair de-staticking stuff. I need to use it all the time. School makes me tense . . . and then my hair just snaps."

"Oh, no. That's okay." He patted his own head but only some of the hair flattened. He took back his helmet. "I like my hair to snap." He walked quickly ahead.

"Wait up!" I followed him into the building.

"Hi, Mrs. Johnson," he called.

She looked up from her desk behind the counter, smiled, and waved at him.

"I'm here too!" I called. "Remember? Sonja Ehret?"

She raised an eyebrow and nodded.

"Teacher's pet," I grumbled at Cole. I took a big inhale of my coffee-bean necklace.

"I don't care about any 'teacher.'" He frowned as he signed the guest log. "I'm here to look after my grandmother. And I'm nice to everyone so that they will be good to her when I leave."

Grouch, I thought and quickly signed in after him as he keyed in the code to unlock the door to the Alzheimer's unit.

The coffee-bean aroma filtered out most of the meatier smell of supper. My necklace was a lifesaver.

Ahead, Marlene and Fred trudged along together heading right for us. Cole leaned back on the door so it would close faster.

"Hold it open!" Fred called to us. "They've changed something."

"We need bread," Marlene added, reaching one hand out.

Blocking the door still, Cole took her hand and gently turned her back the way they had come.

I couldn't stand it anymore: same old sweatpants, this time grey and stained with something orange down the front. "Hi, Fred. Do you mind?" I crouched down and untucked his sweatpant leg from his sock.

"Is that you Diane?" He looked down at me, head tilted.

"No, I'm Sunny."

"Darn. I wish you were Diane."

Cole smirked at this one. *Moron.*

I smiled and tried to sound cheery. "Sorry to disappoint you. Is Diane your daughter?"

"Yes. I'm supposed to go with her today and buy a part for my car."

Cole still watched me. I'd show him just how patient and friendly I could be. "If you could tell me what part, I bet my dad could help me get it for you."

From the side of my eye, I noticed a quick headshake from Cole.

Fred nodded, but then he frowned and his brow furrowed. His eyes moved from side to side quickly like he was looking for a clue to the puzzle in his head.

Too late, I understood my mistake. Playing along with his delusion seemed to have woken him from some peaceful spell. I didn't know what to do.

Marlene rescued us both. "We better keep going," she said, without raising her head. "Stores are going to close."

Incident immediately forgotten, Fred's face smoothed as he looked down and continued along the hall with her.

Another inmate with straggly grey hair sat near a window rocking a naked plastic doll in her arms.

"Hi, Susan," Cole called. "How's the baby?"

Susan just smiled and rocked it some more. She looked happy, like a new mom. It was too weird.

"*Guten tag,* Johann," I said when I saw Mr. Schwartz. But he didn't look up. His eyes were open but he still seemed asleep. "I'm going to feed you dinner today, okay?" I grabbed hold of his wheelchair handles and pushed.

"Hey, Grandma," Cole called out and rushed to a woman with a walker. Even slightly stooped over the handlebars, she looked tall like Cole and she had his golden eyes. Only hers looked dazed. He gave her a kiss and a hug and she smiled.

"You brought your mother." She turned to me. "Nice colour, Claudine. Can you get the hairdresser to do that for me?"

"It's Sunny," I corrected her, deciding I couldn't humour the residents too much. Look how that had confused Fred.

"Sunny is it, Claudine? Let's go for a walk then." His grandma immediately moved towards the glass door that opened onto a courtyard.

"No, Grandma. This is the new volunteer and her *name* is Sunny." Cole winked at me as he caught her elbow and tugged her back. "It's almost suppertime. Maybe we'll walk later. Come to the dining room with us."

I smiled when she said hello the second time.

From around the next corner Jeannette shuffled behind her walker towards us. "Hello there, Gorgeous. What a pretty blouse!"

I looked down at my green V-necked tee. "Thank you, Jeannette. Coming to supper?"

"Well yes. It is my birthday." She grinned as she stepped alongside us, and I wondered if she was trying to put one over on me. Cole's grandma wheeled along at his side.

I pushed Johann's chair into the dining room to his usual spot. A man with shaggy black hair and sideburns was setting up some sound equipment in the corner. He wore a flashy white jumpsuit that looked like it might split when he bent over to plug his microphone in.

"Hello. Here, put this on." Gillian held out some paper party hats.

Cole grabbed one and slipped the elastic around his

chin, placing the cone over his ruffled hair. It was almost an improvement.

I stared at the polka-dotted one she offered me. I hate those hats. They don't sit right, they never fit, the elastic under your neck pinches, and frankly, I spend a lot of time straightening my hair to make it look good. I don't want to wreck it.

"Go on, it's Jeannette, Susan, and my grandma's birthday. We have to celebrate." Cole's eyes, friendly as they seemed, watched me. Was I measuring up?

I shook my head and looked around the room at the old people, sitting with their bodies bent over the tables. Some wore hats, some didn't. I wondered if they even had a say. I sighed. "All these birthdays in one day. Guess that makes this party really special." I took the hat and placed it over my head, pulling the elastic around my chin.

Cole smiled at me and winked. "That should keep your hair from snapping."

The shaggy-haired dude in the corner called into his microphone, "Thank you, thank you very much." Then he began singing an old Elvis song. "Wise men say . . ."

A pretty dismal birthday party if you asked me. One silver, heart-shaped Happy Birthday balloon in the centre of the room and a fairly ordinary meal — chicken or fish sticks with macaroni and beets. I spooned a puddle of red into Johann, then a little brown. He wouldn't take the beige.

"What *is* this?" I asked out loud of no one in particular. Johann kept his lips solidly wedged together.

"That's a dinner roll put through the blender." Cole lifted his eyebrows and nodded. "Try some. Tastes exactly the same."

"No thank you." The shaggy-haired guy strummed and sang but everyone just chewed and swallowed, same as always. I gestured at the sleepy old people around us. "No one seems to be enjoying Elvis."

"Oh no?" Cole suddenly threw his arms open wide and sang along, loud and somewhat flat, looking my way as though he was serenading. "But I . . . can't . . . help . . . falling in love . . . with . . . you."

I couldn't help blushing. "You're an idiot."

When the old people finished their meals, the goth cafeteria worker and a friend brought out a cake. None of the residents sang, only Elvis, the cafeteria workers, Cole, and me. "Happy birthday dear Jeannette, Susan, Fred, and Helen. Happy birthday to you."

No one blew out any candles, nor did anyone get any presents. "So many people born on the same day, what a coincidence." I tasted the cake. It was crumbly and dry and not very sweet.

"Only Jeannette really. They celebrate everyone's birthdays for the whole month today." Cole stuck out his tongue. It was covered in crumbs. "Dietetic. Yuck."

"So they don't even get to celebrate their own day. That's sad." I pushed my cake plate away.

"Yup."

"I'd like to get Jeannette a present. The others, too."

"You don't have to, they won't know."

Elvis started up another song. "Suspicious Minds" it was called.

"Interesting choice," I said, gesturing with my head to him.

"Sing with me," Cole said. "'We can't go on together . . .'"

I rolled my eyes but it didn't stop Cole.

The song ended. "He takes requests," Cole said. "Don't you, Elvis?"

"Uh huh. What would you like, pretty lady?"

For you to stop playing seemed mean. Instead I shrugged. Trouble was, none of the hip hop I liked was really for this crowd. Nor could this dude probably play it.

I looked around at all the grey heads, some nodding as they chewed their safety cake. I watched Cole dab at his grandmother's chin with a napkin. It all made me think of Omi. Wouldn't it be nice if I could be caring for her the way Cole did for his grandmother? And then her favourite song came to me.

"Do you know 'You Are My Sunshine'?"

"Yes, I do. But you're gonna have to sing with me."

He began strumming.

"Oh, I can't sing. You wouldn't want me to —"

"Come on now . . ." He kept strumming. Cole started singing with him.

I winced as I finally joined in. I don't like the sound of my own voice, but couldn't hear it anyway. Like screaming at the airport when the planes land, I was drowned out by fake Elvis, the loud electric strumming, and the clatter of plates as they were collected.

Such a bouncy little song, but it made me sad. I could remember singing it with Omi. I was her sunshine, she had told me. She's the one who started everyone calling me Sunny. But I didn't think I was anyone's sunshine anymore. Especially not my mother's. I had to wipe tears from my cheek.

"You have a beautiful voice," Jeannette told me when it was over. "What a gift."

Wow, I couldn't believe how a compliment from a slightly loony lady made me feel so much better. "Thank you!"

Her gift comment also reminded me about the presents

I wanted to buy, so I asked Cole to help me find out the residents' real birthdays.

"Grandma's lands on your next visit, actually. But you'll go broke if you get things for all of them. Come with me." He took me into his grandma's room and I sat on her flowered couch as he removed an envelope of money from her drawer. "Here's twenty dollars. I wonder if that will be enough. I have something particular in mind."

chapter four

Right away the buzzard starts in on the receptionist. "What did you observe, if anything, about Sonja's visits to Paradise Manor?"

"She didn't like to pay attention to the rules. I had to remind her about signing in and out. She made a face when I asked her to use the sanitizer."

The buzzard sniffs at his notes. "What exactly did she tell you when you asked her to wash her hands?"

"She suggested that the residents needed the sanitizing. That they would pass her their diseases, not the other way around. She also said that they would be lucky if she brought them some illness that would kill them off quicker."

The lady in the kiwi-coloured sweatsuit cringes in her seat.

Okay, maybe I said that, I don't remember. And I shouldn't have — not out loud. I didn't think everyone would be listening and storing my words to judge me with later. But I bet everyone who walks into the Manor thinks it. The residents are ancient and they sleep all the time anyway. Plus I was annoyed about using that sanitizer. I don't think it really kills germs, just the moisture on your skin.

"No further questions. Counsel?"

My lawyer immediately stands up and tilts his head. "Can you tell me, did Sonja often forget to sign in?" His voice sounds bright and cheery, and he smiles as though he's not defending an evil teen.

"She always signed in because she needed proof of her forty hours."

Like that was a crime, I think. Wanting to get my volunteer time counted.

"What about signing out? Did you have to remind her to do that?"

"Yes, most often she forgot to sign out."

Michael nods in acknowledgement. There, great, now the jury knows that I forgot to sign out often. Not just when I supposedly killed someone.

"Were there any other rules she broke?"

"That I personally knew of?"

"Yes. Only those she broke in front of you." He planned for at least one of my hostile witnesses to mention the gifts I gave the seniors.

"Um . . . I know she brought in a pair of sweatpants for one of the patients. But she refused to take them to laundry to label."

Bingo! The chubby guy in stripes sits up.

"What was her explanation for this refusal?"

"She said she wanted to see Fred in new, clean clothing on his birthday at least, and she didn't want to wait. She took out a pen and marked the label with his room number."

The bearded guy with all the pins looks interested too. The guy with the taped-up glasses straightens his head.

"Do you remember whether she signed in on this occasion?"

"As a matter of fact, she said she was just ducking in for a minute and it wasn't her volunteer hour. She didn't sign in or out."

Sometimes I went to Paradise Manor on my own. Truly volunteering. I liked the old people. My lawyer gets that. Only, does the jury? 'Cause I also brought Fred the old stick shift from my father's Mustang. On another day, I brought Susan's naked baby some doll clothes of my own. I had to reattach the doll's head constantly, too, which really meant a lot of pushing and twisting. For Jeannette, I brought a new lipstick and for Cole's grandma, I did something entirely different. Something I got into a lot of trouble over. But the buzzard doesn't show any more journal entries. Maybe if I'd written how Cole begged me to do it, how he said it was the only thing that would make her happy, my lawyer could have used the fourth one.

The Fourth Visit — thirty-two hours left

I'm really making a difference volunteering at Paradise Manor. They celebrated five of the residents' birthdays all on one day. How efficient is that? They hired a tribute singer, and I led the old folks in a few ditties. I also made visits on their real birthdays and did something special for Mrs. Demers. She really enjoyed it. It's like I told you, Mr. Brooks, when you're happy with your hair, it gives you a more positive outlook on life.

I asked my mother for fifty bucks so I could buy the seniors some birthday presents.

"You are very generous with other people's money," Mom said. Her words always sound stiff, disapproving even. Wolfie told me once it was because she had learned Oxford English in school back in Germany. That gave her that upper-crust tone.

"Nobody hires a sixteen-year-old without experience," I grumbled. "What do you expect me to do?"

"Eat your toast. Breakfast is the most important meal of the day."

I bit into an over-crisp corner of bread. I should have hit dad up for the money. Mom likes us to work for everything.

"We came to this country with nothing." She straightened her neck as she poured herself another coffee. People say we look alike, but I didn't see it. My hair is dark like Dad's, though, okay, our eyes are the same pale blue. Mom hadn't dyed her hair since the treatments and there were strands of pale yellow framing her short, curly 'do — exactly where my hair was pink — which made her seem more fragile.

I thought about cutting mine short like Mom's, for Donovan's grad. I'd leave my two long, pink strands. That would make a statement.

"You can come to the condo office. Work there like Wolfgang," Mom suggested. My parents manage five condominium buildings, hiring and paying all the repair and maintenance people. They also attend all owners' meetings and listen to plenty of complaints, as they tell it. "I can teach you to do the bills on the computer."

"In between school, homework, and my volunteer hours, sure. Can I have the money now?"

"No. Tell me one hairdressing salon where the customers pay before they get their hair done?"

I sighed. There it was, her looking down on my job plans. It always came down to that. "You're not a salon, and I need the money to buy the presents in time for a birthday."

My mother just arched an eyebrow. "And then you will never show up to work."

If she seriously needed me to, sure I would. But she didn't seem to know this about me so I didn't argue any further, just finished my toast and went to school. And after school, even without a contribution from Mom, I still went shopping . . . with Donovan. We browsed the men's formal-wear shop in the corner of the mall. He wanted to really stand out for this grad, his third. Maybe a kilt?

I wrinkled my nose.

Maybe a white tuxedo instead of the standard, silky lapelled black one?

I shook my head. "You know what? Once I get a dress, we can try to coordinate your outfit, Donny. Let's go look at track pants."

"Why?" he squealed. "Who wears track pants?"

"My brother Wolfie when he works out. And it's all the old guys ever wear at Paradise Manor. Look over there! The sales rack in front of Sport X. It's a sidewalk sale, two for one." I dragged Donovan over by the arm. "What size would you wear, Don?"

"I wouldn't wear any."

"Medium?" I held up a pair against him. "One black pair for Johann and one navy pair for Fred."

"Do you have any money?" he asked.

"Ten bucks left from my allowance. Don't you have any?"

"Oh, Sunny!" He rolled his eyes. "Go into the shop and look at shoes for yourself." He laced his fingers through each other and stretched them.

The track pants weren't for me, they were for the old people. Charity, not stealing, I reasoned with myself nervously. I drifted to the shoe wall. A clerk in a referee's striped shirt approached. *Jacob*, his name tag read.

"Anything I can help you with?" he asked.

I shook my head. "I don't really jog."

"Then these cross trainers might be for you." He took down a pair of striped, red-suede runners. "They're on sale, too."

A sporty look without that industrial functionality jogging shoes always seemed to have. I couldn't resist and tried them on. "They're great, really." I looked past him to the sweatpants rack. Donovan had disappeared already. "Sorry, I'll have to come back for them another day."

Jacob smiled at me "Sure. Want me to put them aside?"

I felt bad. If I'd had money, I would have bought them. But then I would have paid for those sweatpants, too. "No, that's okay." I walked away quickly.

Never again, I promised myself. That was the last time I even shopped with Donovan, just in case. For the final present, I needed to consult with Alexis anyway.

Alexis agreed to help me. So on Saturday, we walked together to the drugstore to buy the dye for Mrs. Demers. It was a perfect October day, warm but with none of that stickiness that makes your hair droop. On the way, Alexis told me about her volunteer placement at the shelter and how she was photographing all the animals there so that they could put their pictures on the Net and adopt them out faster.

"Cool. So it's not all poopy-scooping for dogs. Do you keep some pictures for yourself? A souvenir?"

"No, I didn't think of that. But next time I'll download some on a memory stick now that you mentioned it."

Then I told her about the mass birthday at Paradise Manor. "After the cake, this paunchy dude in a jumpsuit and a wig played all these songs and only Cole sang."

"Back it up. Who is this Cole person? Is he cute?"

I frowned when I pictured him in my head. "Nah . . . at least not like Donovan. He's more the sweet kind. He's not volunteering for his graduation requirement. He's just there to visit with his grandma. It breaks my heart."

"Oh, now I get it. She's the one you're buying the hair dye for."

I stopped walking for a second. "There's nothing to get, Alexis. It's her birthday on Monday, that's all. You know I'm going to the prom with Donovan." My voice came out sharpish.

She put out her hands like she was shielding herself.

Reaching the edge of the sidewalk first, I lifted my foot to step onto the street.

"Careful!" Alexis flung her arm across my waist. "There's a car turning."

Tsk. "Talking on the cell phone. She should get a ticket." When it was safe, we crossed the street to the super-sized pharmacy. "Then Cole more or less forced me to sing along."

"With your voice?" Alexis lifted an eyebrow.

"Exactly! After I told him how tone deaf I was, too." We walked to the first aisle where all the hair product was kept. I picked up a box of a dark red shade. "But I did finally join in."

"You didn't! Isn't that red too dark, Sunny?"

"Not on white hair." I frowned. "But it's a permanent. There must be something else." I picked up a copper-coloured can and checked the label. It was a mousse called Beat and the instructions said it washed out in eight to ten shampoos. "All those old folks made me miss Omi and I sang her favourite song. Jeannette said my voice was a gift."

"I guess she's pretty deaf too. What about this shade?"

She handed me a can of Beat with Electric Cherry printed across the lid.

"Yup, that will do the trick." We took the mousse to the front checkout. "Jeannette isn't deaf. She just likes me."

"Is that the one who always compliments your clothes? Ones you're not even wearing?"

"So what? She's confused. She really brightens when she sees me. Makes me feel good." I handed the money to the clerk. "And now I can actually do someone's hair. It's not quite like co-opping at the salon, but it's not bad."

Back then I thought it was a lovely gesture, but now I knew it would be turned against me during the trial.

chapter five

The next person the old buzzard calls up is Gillian Halliday. I relax in my chair. She thought I was a natural with the old people. She will be on my side. There couldn't possibly be anything wrong that she would say about me.

Gillian has to swear in and state her occupation like everyone else. Today she wears her hair pulled back in a conservative bun, no happy-go-lucky braids and beads. Better for the fashion-dysfunctional jury anyway.

The buzzard checks his notes. "What kind of duties do you assign volunteers at Paradise Manor?

"Mostly feeding the residents and helping them with activities. The old people get lonely and they like the youngsters comin' around and chattin' with them."

"And how did Sonja Ehret fit in with the duties?"

"She wanted to do everything just so. She liked to fix the old folks' collars and make their sweaters straight. She combed some of the ladies' hair for me."

"Could you describe any other hairdressing activities she might have performed for them?"

"Well now, if you're bringin' up that hair-dyin' incident, that was just a misunderstandin'. She was just bein' nice to

Mrs. Demers and didn't know she needed to ask permission before doin' anythin' with her hair colour."

"Would you explain exactly what she did to Mrs. Demers?"

"You have to understand that some of the ladies think they're teenagers themselves and they all want to be cute like Sunny. Mrs. Demers liked the pink streaks Sunny has in her hair. She asked Sunny if she could have stripes like that too."

"And what did Sonja do?"

"Well, she bought a temporary colour and combed some through Mrs. Demers's hair."

"Where would she have gotten the money, do you know?"

"Mrs. Johnson said she stole it from Mrs. Demers's special drawer but —"

"Objection. Hearsay," my lawyer calls.

"Sustained," the judge answers. "The jury should disregard that last answer."

Oh sure, you can tell them to disregard it, but don't they all now believe that I'm a thief?

The buzzard continues. "Could you describe Mrs. Demers's hair after?"

"Mrs. Demers really liked the pink. It was just her daughter-in-law who got angry. She thought Sunny was makin' a fool of the old lady."

"But how did you think it looked?"

"The pink on the white didn't appear the way Sunny's streaks do — she having the dark brown hair and all. Mrs. Demers looked like she had candy-cane hair."

"No further questions." The buzzard swoops back down into his seat.

"Does the defence wish to question Miss Halliday?" the judge calls.

"Yes, Your Honour." My lawyer stands up and smiles at Gillian. "Miss Halliday, how would you characterize Sonja's relationship with the residents at Paradise Manor?"

"They liked her, she bein' young and pretty."

"And how would you describe her attitude to them? You said she straightened their clothing? How did she react to their dementia, for example?"

"She treated them very seriously. If they asked her questions, she really thought hard to give them honest answers. She brought them little treats. And she wanted them to have choices. Her and Cole, they were always talkin' about that."

The jury member in the plaid shirt gives a nervous *heh*. It sounds like the first beat of a laugh. Did letting them have choices seem dangerous to him?

My lawyer ignores it. "You said she should have asked permission to colour Mrs. Demers's hair. But Mrs. Demers asked to have pink streaks. What was Mrs. Demers's grandson's attitude and reaction towards the hair colouring?"

"He helped her because he thought it would bring his grandma pleasure."

"So I'm confused then. Help me out with something. If her grandson and Mrs. Demers gave permission, how did Sonja come to be reprimanded for the incident?"

"Well, Mrs. Johnson insisted we had to inform Cole's mother and when she saw the hair for herself, she blew up."

"And how often would you say Cole's mother usually came to visit?"

"That was the first time this year. She never visits."

My lawyer frowns and rubs his chin. "So Helen Demers

wanted her hair streaked and enjoyed the pink colour?"

"Yes."

"And her daughter-in-law would have never known if Paradise Manor hadn't called her. Is that correct?"

Gillian shifts in her chair as she looks towards Mrs. Johnson on the other side of the room. "Yes. That is correct."

"No further questions."

Cole's mom called what I did to Helen's hair vandalism. Cole said she'd yelled about it in front of his grandmother and got her all upset. "She can't help herself, though," he explained after I was lectured by Mrs. Johnson. "Mom overreacts to anything to do with Grandma's Alzheimer's 'cause she can't cope." He made me feel sorry for his mother so I let it go and just did what Mr. Brooks told me I had to in order to continue with the project. The jury could read how nicely I played along if they could just read my next journal entry.

The Fifth Visit — thirty hours left

I apologized to Mrs. Johnson for streaking Helen's hair just as you told me to, Mr. Brooks. I promised her I'd never do anything like that again and she let me back to volunteer. As usual, Johann barely had anything to eat because I fed him slowly as she'd asked and he fell asleep in the middle. Since it was warm enough, we took a few of the residents outside after supper. Not so many UV rays at that time of the day. It wasn't easy to push Johann's wheelchair out, but in the end I think he enjoyed his time in the sun.

No matter what Claudine Demers said, Helen's candy-striped hair made her look very cool. Despite the hair perk, though, she had a very bad day. She suddenly couldn't walk and Cole had to borrow the Manor wheelchair to get her to dinner. She didn't talk much during the meal either, but when I noticed her staring at Johann's brownie, I slipped it to her.

"You're not supposed to give Mrs. Demers anything with sugar," the goth cafeteria worker told me.

Helen had already taken two bites and smiled.

"I'm so sorry," I lied to her. "I had no idea. I won't do it again, Sheila," I added, reading her name tag.

Sheila didn't accept my apology even though I looked her directly in the eye and acted sincere. "Better not," she grumbled at me as she collected the trays of half-eaten food.

As I wheeled the sleeping Johann back towards the hall, I met up with Cole.

"Do you want to take them into the courtyard?" Cole asked. "Maybe it will cheer Grandma up. She always liked fall."

"Sure. Be nice for all of us." Cole looked like he could use some cheering up too. "Want me to swipe some more brownies for her?"

Cole winked and shook his head. "Not now." His eyes looked behind me and when I turned I noticed Sheila clearing the table close to us.

"Just kidding." I grinned and winked back at him.

He led the way out towards the door that opened onto a rectangular court, protected by the four walls of the building. No wind reached us, and the air felt warm. Yellow and purple mums grew in the flower beds.

We parked the old people across from a wooden bench so we could sit too. Cole sprawled across the seat, his right leg touching mine.

I shifted away. "Too bad we can't see the coloured leaves from here."

"I could have tried for permission to take them to the front, but Mrs. Johnson's not happy with us right now. She probably would have said no."

I shrugged. "They're both asleep. I guess it doesn't matter."

"Guess not." His arm drifted across the back of the bench behind my head. There was nowhere left for me to shift. "No matter what, I'm glad you streaked Grandma's hair. Made her happy for that moment."

I leaned back against the bench, and his arm, closing my eyes to enjoy the last glow of summer. "Yeah, that was something." I chuckled. "Jeannette wants me to do hers too now."

"Me too." Cole let his hand rest on my shoulder.

"You're close to your grandma. It's sweet." I opened my eyes again.

He smiled. "She looked after me when I was little."

"Mine did too."

Cole played with my hair, lifting it so he could touch my neck. He leaned closer to me.

I looked into his eyes. Warm gold. He liked me, I knew he did.

His lips drew to mine.

Johann groaned in his wheelchair suddenly, startling me. I pulled away. What was I doing? Cole was kind and cute in a different way than Donovan. Still no reason to let him kiss me. His grandmother still slept peacefully. I took a breath. "What ever happened to her?" I asked him. "I mean, how did you know she had Alzheimer's?"

Cole cleared his throat and sat up on the bench. "First she locked herself out of the house a few times 'cause she couldn't find her key. We didn't think too much of it."

"Anyone can lose a key," I agreed, putting my hand on his shoulder.

Cole nodded and frowned. "Only then it got worse. One day she tried to pay her bill at the restaurant with a plumber's business card."

"Oh! What did the doctor say?"

Cole shrugged. "He gave her some pills."

"Did they help at all?"

He shook his head. "The next time she went to the store she couldn't find her way home." He kicked at the edge of the walkway. "When Dad and I found her, she cried and promised it would never happen again. But Mom couldn't give up her job to look after her. And Dad wouldn't take the chance."

"So she's here," I finished for him.

"No. She went on a waiting list. She disappeared three more times. The last time, she was hit by a car. Mom refused to take her back home. Grandma stayed in the hospital till a spot opened up at Paradise Manor."

I nodded. "She seems better than most of the others, though."

"I don't know. I think she's slipping. Not walking is bad," Cole told me.

"Really, you don't think your mom's fuss about the hair put her in a funk?"

He shook his head. "No. It's the disease progressing."

"I'm sorry, Cole." I touched his arm. "But at least you visit her. There's nothing else you can do."

"Well, yes. There is something else. And she made me promise to do it when the disease progressed too far."

chapter six

The next person the buzzard calls to the stand is Sheila Swanson, the cafeteria goth. She fixes me with her evil stare. We all know where this is heading.

He asks her what kind of behaviour I exhibited towards the seniors when she was around.

Sheila shifts in the chair and looks at me with a satisfied smile. "Sonja rushed Johann, that is Mr. Schwartz, when he ate and didn't seem too concerned when food stuck in his throat. He was only supposed to be eating mashed but she tried to give him solids."

"And her attitude, in general, to staff?" The buzzard flips a page of his notes. Of course, he's scanning ahead at all the answers she's already given him.

Sheila puffs up indignantly. "She always seemed to blame us . . . for everything from dietary restrictions to the patients' inability to choose their own meals. And she never took any of our rules seriously."

There's a nervous laugh cough from the guy in plaid. He probably doesn't like diets either. Hopefully he's on my side.

The buzzard fixes Sheila with his window-cleaner eyes. "Can you describe Sunny and Cole's relationship?"

"Oh, he had a crazy crush on her. And we saw them holding hands sometimes." She says this as though it was part of the crime: we liked each other so I must have tried to choke his grandma.

"And what behaviour and attitude did you observe in Cole towards his grandmother?"

"Like Sonja, he tried to sneak his grandmother sweets, which her diabetic condition did not allow." She smiles at me again, thin lips stretched out long and triumphant.

"In your opinion . . ." he says, in a loud voice with a weighty pause after, "did you feel he was deliberately sabotaging her health?"

"Objection!" My lawyer leaps to his feet. The front row jurors seem to sit up in attention. "The Crown is openly asking for an unsubstantiated feeling."

"Sustained," the judge answers.

The jury looks confused. The guy in the back scratches his beard. The man in the plaid shirt coughs nervously. *Heh, heh.*

At least Cole and I never deliberately tried to sabotage his grandmother's happiness!

The woman in the stained T-shirt at the front folds her arms. What conclusion is she drawing? If the jury only knew Cole the way I did from the volunteer hours, they would understand how deeply he cared about his grandmother.

The fat man rubs at his forehead, back and forth, like he's trying to clean something off. Here in the courtroom, my lawyer can object all he wants and the judge can sustain every objection, but that buzzard planted an idea in their minds: that Cole wanted to kill his grandma. And the buzzard's already suggested I carried out this plan in his opening statement. This will stay in the jurors' minds, there's really no recalling it.

The Sixth Visit — twenty-eight hours left

Miss Halliday asked me and the other volunteer, Cole, if we would come in for the weekend Halloween Party instead of our usual feeding shift. I dressed up as a princess so I wouldn't frighten anyone and Cole dressed up as a scarecrow. We made sure the residents got their treats. The neat thing is that some of the residents' grandchildren came in their costumes. The old people really loved the kids.

Orange and black streamers hung along the walls. Bunches of matching balloons were weighted down to tables by mini pumpkins. No dangling skeletons, googly-eyed witches, or floating heads. Cole explained that some of the scarier Halloween décor might cause the old folks to hallucinate, so they had to keep it low-key. Likewise the staff was dressed up mostly as clowns or dolls — no Zombies or brides of Frankenstein. Gillian made a great puppy dog.

The truth about the party was that, like the birthday celebration, it felt lame. Not that many people came — the staff, a few adults, and five kids. The residents didn't dress up. Well, really, did it matter? Halloween wasn't exactly an adult holiday.

I was glad to be there, in costume, killing volunteer hours and sneaking in some fun with Cole.

"Look at the cute baby cat," Susan yelled as she pointed to a toddler dressed as a lion.

The baby's face, circled by a brown mane, crumpled at

her loud voice. Then his mouth opened into a full-scale wail and his mom had to scoop him away to the balloons, jiggling and shushing to try to calm him.

"Aw man, who cut the cheese?" a short ghost grumbled.

The ghost's dad tapped his head and told him not to be so rude.

I grinned at Cole as I lifted my coffee-bean necklace to my nose. Nothing worked better, although at supper when we usually volunteered, the smell of meatloaf and broccoli or other cooked meats and vegetables covered the odour too.

"Excuse me." A little girl with a green face and a peaked hat tugged at my dress. "How many cookies are we allowed?"

Oh gawd, tell me she didn't think I worked here. "Ten," I answered.

Grinning, she grabbed up a handful from a plate on the table.

"You must be a good witch," her twin said as she snatched up the rest.

"She's Glinda," Cole agreed, tipping his hat. "And I'm the scarecrow." He picked up another plate of cookies and we visited with the old folks parked around the walls and on the couches.

"Thank you," Jeannette said as she took an orange-iced shortbread pumpkin from his plate. She waved it at me. "Those pants look so nice on you. I bet you make a good traveller."

I looked down at myself, confused. What was she seeing? I was wearing a sparkly white wedding gown I'd picked up from Value Village, not really a great travelling outfit. But Jeannette's compliments seemed so specific, in a random way. Was my way of seeing things or hers the right one? Did it matter? "Thank you, Jeannette. I think you could travel well in your outfit, too."

Jeannette was wearing a burgundy dress with brown sweatpants underneath. Bag lady fashion, really. She smiled back radiantly. "Thank you."

"Happy Halloween." I raised my cookie in a toast.

She raised hers.

From an old-fashioned boom box on the shelf a song began to play. "I did the mash, I did the monster mash."

"You there, little boy," Jeannette suddenly snapped. She grabbed a short pirate with a skull-and-crossbones kerchief on his head. "Why don't you dance to the nice music?"

The little pirate boy looked back towards his mother, who shrugged.

"Turn it up! Turn it up!" Jeannette waved her hand in the air. I flipped the volume knob to the right.

Immediately, the pirate threw himself onto the floor into a Cossack kick. After a few energetic moments of that, he switched into some kind of twirl while he leaned on one hand. Breakdancing? And from there he straightened into a slow-motion moonwalk. None of the movements went with the beat or the music but he grinned as he danced and Jeannette actually grinned wider.

"Bravo! More, more!" She clapped.

It was awkward. The little boy looked helplessly around, like he didn't want to keep going. So Cole started dancing alongside him in a sloppy scarecrow jig. No rhythm. *Nothing smooth about him, so unlike Donovan,* I thought, shaking my head.

He held out his hand for me and I sighed, not wanting to dance this hokey pokey but knowing there was no arguing with Cole. I grabbed his hand and pirouetted into my best fairy plié. Silly dancing, nothing matching anything else: jig changing into a waltz, a breakdance into a twist.

At one point I collided with Cole and the crash turned into a hug. He smiled at me. I couldn't help smiling back, but still pulled away.

When the song finished, I immediately volunteered to get Jeannette a glass of Boo juice — a punch the colour of berries or fresh blood, depending on your mood.

"This is for your grandma." Batgirl (aka the cafeteria goth) handed Cole a digestive biscuit and a plastic glass full of what looked like apple juice. "Have to keep those sugar levels down."

He brought them to her. She looked very much out of this world, slumped in her now permanent wheelchair. Even her pink streaks did nothing to liven up her face. It hadn't just been a single bad day for her as everyone hoped. Imagine that: one day just forgetting how to walk.

"I don't know why they don't let her enjoy herself at Halloween at least," he told me as he held up the plain-looking rectangle to her mouth.

I strolled over to Johann, a few chairs down along the wall, taking a cookie plate with me. He didn't have any family visiting, in costume or not.

"*Was ist loss?*" he asked me, his forehead crinkled with anxiety.

"Halloween," I told him, offering him the plate.

He winced at me, still confused.

"Oktoberfest?" I tried again.

He nodded, looking satisfied and took a shortbread, crumbling it against his mouth.

"Easy. Taste some." He was used to mushed food but the cookie was too delicious to miss. I opened my mouth and pretended to eat something.

The next time he actually opened his mouth. I shoved a small piece in. He didn't seem to know what to do with it for a while. He didn't chew or swallow. But his mouth stretched into a smile. Maybe it had melted in his mouth. Good.

Marlene and Fred shuffled through the recreation room and puppy dog Gillian tried unsuccessfully to get them to sit down.

"We're out of bread," I heard Marlene say.

Both Fred's pant legs were tucked into his socks today. I hated the look but at least his legs matched. Around the room most of the residents sat slumped, staring out expressionless. A few slept. Did they really need or appreciate a Halloween party?

The pirate and his mom left. The witch twins kissed their grandma goodbye. The lion baby refused to hug Marlene, and her mother had to finally leave with him. The ghost drifted after his dad.

In the corner, Susan stood alone rocking her doll.

I asked Cole what he thought of the party.

"Some kids came. The old people love them." He shrugged. "If they enjoy it for a second, it's still good. People with Alzheimer's have to live in the moment. Moments are their lifetime."

Definitely there was that one moment with Jeannette during the dancing and maybe half of one when Johann enjoyed his cookie. Still. One second of enjoyment didn't seem enough for a lifetime. Same as those last five minutes with Helen Demers shouldn't have destroyed my life either.

chapter seven

The judge leans over and looks at my lawyer. "Does the defence wish to question the witness?"

"Yes, Your Honour." Michael McCann stands. No fussing with his notes, no playing with his tie. The jury members relax back into their seats. "Mrs. Swanson, what would you say is the attitude of most of the visitors to Paradise Manor?"

"Some are very grateful for the care their loved ones are given."

The jury member with the broken glasses starts cleaning them. One of the goatee twins strokes his beard. There's a ring piercing his chin, too. Oh my gawd!

"And how do the others react?" Michael asks brightly, giving her his teddy-bear eyes.

"Well, some are sad about the state the patient is in."

He lifts his hands as though asking for help. "And how does that sadness manifest itself?"

"They can be angry."

He leans forward. "With the patient?"

"No, with the staff. They can question caregiving, routines, rules."

He nods. "The way Sonja Ehret did?"

Sheila frowns as though caught in something and nods.

"Could you respond out loud for the record?"

"Yes, the way Sonja did. But she wasn't related to the patients. There were no emotions involved for her."

Objection, I think. You don't have to be related to a person to care about them.

"No further questions," my lawyer says.

Heh, heh. The guy in the plaid shirt coughs. *So there,* it sounds like.

I did too have emotions about those people, I want to yell at him. *Look in my journal!* If they kept reading it, they would see. I cared about the patients and sometimes they really wiped me out.

The Seventh Visit — twenty-six hours left

Mr. Brooks, my volunteer hours are giving me a better understanding of what caregivers and families experience. One of the patients became anxious and I tried to calm her down. It didn't work and she looked like she was going to hit me, so I had to leave for a while. I didn't think I could even come back, but I did. I'm going to try harder to be nicer to her because it's not her fault her brain is shutting down. I'm trying really hard with all of them.

It was warm and sunny that day, great weather for November! I actually rode my bike to Paradise Manor. Because I didn't have to wait around for a bus, it took way less time than usual to get there and the sound of the swishing rust-coloured leaves along the road put me in a great mood. The last few blocks I rode alongside Cole. Also a mood booster.

"You should wear a helmet," Cole told me when we locked the bikes to the rack in front of the home.

"Look at your hair, look at mine," I told him as I shook my head and raked through it with my fingers.

"Yours is . . . great," he said, staring at me for a second.

"Thank you." My hair is thick and lustrous (from Dad's side). I smiled and looked back into his eyes. "Here, why don't you let me fix yours. It's my thing."

"Oh, fine. Go crazy." He put his chin down obediently so his hair faced me.

I took out my Smooth, rubbed some in my palms, and ran my hands over his hair. I flicked some into spikes. "There. Nice."

He lifted his head again and I saw a perfect reflection of me in the gold of his eyes. He caught my wrist. "Thank you," he murmured.

"You're welcome." I pulled my arm back again but it tingled all the way up from where he had touched. We strolled into the Manor through the sliding doors. I used the hand sanitizer, without a lecture, and signed in. Cole followed my example and then keyed in the code.

"Hello there, Gorgeous. That's a nice dress." Jeannette shuffled up to me.

Cole hung back.

I was wearing tight, brown leggings so as not to get any clothing parts caught in the bicycle chain. "Thank you."

"Can you help me get out of here? I'm lost and I don't know anyone." Jeannette shuffled closer, her eyes dazed today.

Standing in front of the bookshelf-camouflaged door, I shrugged and shook my head. "Sorry, I don't know the way either."

"You must," her voice dropped low.

"Is it over around that corner?" This was the way the nurses did it — distracted, delayed, changed the subject, lied. It didn't feel good.

"You have to help me," Jeannette pleaded. "None of my friends are here."

Cole touched my elbow, warning me or letting me know he was there to help me escape.

I brushed him off. Didn't I know how to handle Jeannette? Hadn't I watched the nurses and aides enough times? "Well, maybe you have to make new friends," I suggested in a bubbly voice, giving her the line all adults use on kids when they move into a new neighbourhood or change schools.

"Don't be so stupid!" Jeannette snarled, baring her teeth. "Tell me the way out."

"Sor-ry." I backed away.

She pushed her walker towards me again. "Wipe that smile from your face. It's hideous. You make me crazy." Her face closed in on mine. Did she intend to bite me?

Cole stepped closer.

I stopped smiling.

"You're ugly." She grabbed my shirt now. "Why do you keep me here?"

I yanked back sharply.

"Jeannette," Cole spoke to her as she reached again, her fingers bent like hooks. "Don't touch," he said gently. He pushed her hand away.

While he stepped between us, I turned to the door and keyed in the code at world-record speed.

Cole chased after me through the passageway. "Don't go! Sunny, don't!" He caught up to me just as I was heading through the double-door exit. He swung me into his arms and I started crying.

"Come on, Sunny. She's crazy. She didn't mean any of that."

"But I thought she liked me." Just the way my grandmother did. Omi also made a big production over how pretty I was or how nice my clothes were.

"Like you?" Cole said. "I'd say she loves you."

I looked up and stopped crying. "No she doesn't. She hasn't known me long enough."

"For Alzheimer's patients, a moment is their lifetime. You're someone who is nice to her. She likes the way you look. I would say, in her own way, she loves you."

I shook my head. "I do my best with them. I don't know how to handle her anymore." I felt more tears sliding down my face. Why did I care about some old biddy? It's just that I liked hearing her say nice things about me, even if they were about articles of clothing I wasn't wearing.

"No one knows what to do with them. That's always a problem." Cole led me by the hand to the lobby to one of the couches next to the fake fireplace. "Sit down here a second. Let me get you a tea. Just don't move."

By the couch lay a big ceramic English bulldog. I sat down and touched the dog's head. I didn't know what the decorators thought when they were accessorizing this place — fake dogs don't make you feel better. I picked up a clothing catalogue from the table. *Independence, dignity, and fashion,* it advertised on the cover. All opposites of what the residents got when they moved in here. I flipped through. Inside were full-colour spreads of a special accessible clothing line. Boxy, easy-wash casuals with plenty of Velcro on the back to make putting the stuff on or tearing it off easy.

My worst nightmare. I'd be angry if I were Jeannette, too.

Cole rushed back out in that moment, carrying my tea in a brown plastic cup. He handed it to me. "I just guessed how you like it." A wedge of lemon floated on top.

"I don't even drink tea," I answered, sipping. But the warmth of the cup against my hands felt nice, and the hot tea refreshed me. "What did you tell Gillian?"

"I didn't see her. I just spoke to the cafeteria lady and said you needed a minute."

"Thanks."

"The residents probably get to the staff too. Those seniors can be nasty."

I shook my head and sipped some more tea. "I don't think I can face Jeannette anymore. It's my fault. I shouldn't have told her she needed to make new friends."

Cole smiled. "Don't worry. She can't carry a grudge." He chuckled then. "The good thing about Alzheimer's patients is they're so good at forgetting."

I laughed, too. "You don't think she'll still be mad at me?"

"Finish your tea and then let's go back and see."

I slowly sipped up the last mouthful.

"Ready?"

I shrugged my shoulders and stood up.

"Here. Let me just do this." He reached over and kissed me, gently, sweetly on the lips.

"What's that for?" I mused.

"For me, what do you think?" He paused for a moment. "Honestly, it's just 'cause you care so much."

I smiled. He thought I was a good person. That meant a lot to me.

Together we passed into the lockup ward again. I saw Jeannette ahead but marched forward anyway. What if she wanted me to help her escape again? I wished I could take her away. How could she live like this? But I couldn't help her leave; I was stuck here myself. I had to complete my volunteer hours no matter what.

As we drew nearer, her sharp brown eyes greeted mine. "Hello, Gorgeous. Those are lovely pants. Have you been travelling far?"

chapter eight

"The court will recess till tomorrow at ten a.m." The judge lifts himself from his chair, gown floating all around him. The man with the clipboard and the two witnesses who hung around, the receptionist, and the cafeteria worker rise as he leaves out his side door. They stay standing as my parents and I exit too.

Mom says goodbye and makes a dash for her car. She's got an appointment with her doctor; if she doesn't hit any traffic she should just make it.

Dad and I drive back to the condo building where the office is. The lobby has high-gloss marble walls and a spectacular water fountain. The three offices where my parents work are painted in autumn green. I helped choose the shade. They're furnished with rosewood desks and chairs and huge flat-screened computers. In my mother's office, where Wolfgang is working, there are school photos of my brother and me on the desk. On the wall is a large print of a woman carrying a young girl on the beach. "You and your mother," Dad had said when he bought it.

Michael McCann said it would be best if both of my parents came to court. The judge would think better of me, my upbringing, and my chances for rehabilitation, God forbid the jury should find me guilty and he have to decide on a sentence. But both my parents want to be there anyway, even if Michael hadn't suggested it.

Still, they can't lose any more business. As it is, the last condo unit they bid on chose another management company. Lots of seniors live in condos; the board couldn't afford to hire elder killers.

My parents need to keep earning a lot of money to pay my lawyer. They hired the best because I needed him. They also promised to pay the court fifty thousand dollars if I don't follow my bail conditions. Otherwise I'd be sitting in jail until the trial was over.

I hate all the pressure I've caused. I should have gone to jail instead, made it easier for them.

Dad orders Thai food over the phone: two dishes of pad thai, one of steamed pork dumplings, a mango chicken, and a seaweed glass-noodle salad. Then we listen to the day's events from Wolfie's point of view: which service people came to which buildings as promised, how the garage was leaking in the Empress building, when the next of board-of-directors meeting for the Princess building could be scheduled.

"How did it go for you, Sunny?" my brother asks. He's short and broad like Dad but has Mom's blond hair.

"I don't know. People repeated things about me that make me sound so bad. And I didn't get a chance to explain. I should have just pleaded guilty."

"Don't say that," Wolfie says, grabbing my hand.

"Well, it would be easier on all of you, too. You wouldn't have to work at night to keep up."

"We always work nights." My father reaches his arm over my shoulders. "Did we ever complain, Sunny? I will spend my money on lawyers any time to prove you are innocent."

The food arrives. By the time Dad has paid, and we each have helped ourselves, Mom comes in silent and pale.

Something's wrong.

She doesn't even reach for a plate. Just sits down and massages her forehead with her hand.

"Did they find something?" I ask, voicing everyone's fear.

Mom squeezes her eyes closed and nods.

Dad puts his arm around her and waits for her to explain.

"It's probably nothing. But I will have an ultrasound tomorrow early, before court and then . . . we will see for sure."

"You have to eat," Dad says and dishes out some pad thai for her.

She smiles at him.

I pile the seaweed salad I saved for her on her plate. Our favourite. We discovered it when we heard that it was packed with anticarcinogens.

My mother takes a forkful and then rests. She turns to Wolfgang. "Did Alexis bring Sunny's homework?"

My big brother nods.

The ordinary stuff, that's all my mother can focus on. I get that. The office for them and school for me. So I use the lemon Wetnaps that came with the Thai and head for Dad's desk to work as hard as I can on my assignments. I have to do brilliantly at school now, to make up for all this trouble I've caused. To help Mom feel better when she's so sick.

That night I find it hard to sleep and when I finally do, my grandmother comes to me in a dream. Bald from her cancer treatments, she grins at me with flashing teeth and bright blue eyes.

In the dream, I cry out and back away. But then her grin

softens into a beautiful smile and she starts singing softly. It is a German lullaby, one she sang to me a hundred times or more, whenever I was sad or afraid. She translated and explained it once. Something about how God counts the stars in the sky to make sure none are missing. How he also knows about you and loves you too.

In the dream she finishes singing and reaches out to hug me. "*Ich liebe dich auch.*" I love you too. I hug her back.

The Eighth Visit — twenty-four hours left

There's no way I can interview any of the residents for Remembrance Day, the way you suggested, Mr. Brooks. Of the thirty-two residents in the lockup ward, only one seems to have served in the armed forces, judging from the photos displayed in the windows in front of all their rooms. Most of the pictures show very young, beautiful people. If the old people only remember the past and confuse it with the present, what do they think when they see themselves in the mirror? I'll think of something else, though.

At school we had a Remembrance Day assembly and a two-minute silence at eleven o'clock. With my parents being German, all the talk of soldiers giving their lives so the rest of us could have freedom hits kind of a sour note. Our whole family wears poppies. "Good public relations," Dad says, but two of my great-grandfathers fought for the Nazis and died in prisoners-of-war camps. Mom usually says something like, "Good young boys died on both sides." Nothing you want to spend even two minutes reminiscing about. Instead, I caught up with Alexis during the official "silence" and got a detention. Mr. Brooks let me serve it at lunchtime so I could still volunteer at the home that afternoon.

After school, even though the air was nippy, I rode my bike over to Paradise Manor, catching up to Cole for the last block again. Cole wasn't hot like Donovan. He was awkward, and a bad dancer and singer, and the golden eyes didn't make up for all that. But each time we met at the Manor, I found myself lighting up.

When we arrived, I used my Smooth on him just like last time, forcing a few cute little spikes into his messy helmet hair. I felt my face warming.

As we strolled through the ward, a young woman approached us, looking confused. She couldn't be a new resident — she seemed too active and determined and definitely too young.

"Can we help you? Are you looking for someone?" Cole asked.

"Yes. My father. He's not in his room or in the recreation centre. But he usually walks around with a woman."

"We saw Fred with Marlene when we came in," I told her.

"Fred? No, my father's name is Walter. About this tall," she showed a height just above her own shoulders, "and the woman is my height. They're not married. They've just sort of latched onto each other."

"Just like Fred and Marlene," I explained. "I don't know your dad but I'll keep an eye out for him."

She continued past us.

"Can you just walk with me?" I asked Cole. "I want to look at all the photos in the residents' display windows. To see if I can find any veterans."

"Sure. I wouldn't mind knowing more about the old folks, too," Cole said as we continued the hall circuit side by side. "I've seen another couple walking together. Probably that guy was Walter. Just didn't see them today."

Our fingers accidentally brushed and my hand tingled from the touch. But Cole didn't grab on. The Manor kind of shook the ground beneath my feet and made me feel wobbly. I suddenly needed to hold on to him too, like Marlene did to Fred. So I took his hand. He smiled at me.

We slowed down at the door to each room. Many of the windows were empty. Most contained a wedding photo and a family portrait. Marlene looked blissfully happy in the arms of a slick-haired groom. In other shots she held the hands of two children, smiling, on the verge of laughing even. Jeannette's contained a portrait photo of a beautiful woman with a '60s-style pageboy cut. In front of her face she held a Nikon camera.

"Jeannette was a photographer?" I asked.

Cole shrugged his shoulders. "Maybe."

I sighed. Alexis wanted to take pictures for a living too. It was a cool job.

Susan's display window showed a dark-haired woman with a white, square cap marked by a black stripe. She held a newborn baby in her arms. "Wow. It looks like Susan was a pediatric nurse." Another great job.

Fred's photo showed him in the full red uniform of the Royal Canadian Mounted Police. Poor Fred, now he wandered the halls in stained sweatpants. From the photo, he looked directly into my eyes. His lips twisted slightly, as though he was amused about something he saw in me. I fidgeted with the sides of my hair.

Photographer, nurse, police officer — good jobs, worth-while, useful people, now all more or less turned into wheel-chair gnomes parked along the hall.

Johann wore a uniform in his photo too. "Is that a German uniform?" I asked Cole.

"Sure is," he answered.

"Guess he wouldn't have much to say about the war, anyway."

"No. Although who knows what he's always ranting about, it could be some battle. Hi, Susan," he called.

She sat in a chair near the recreation room, a strange grin on her face. She half-covered her fully clothed baby doll with her own sweater as she rocked it.

"Those aren't her regular glasses," I told Cole.

"You're right. Hers are silver-rimmed. Those frames are purple."

It was almost time for us to head for the dining room, but we split up to search for her glasses anyway. No luck.

In between feeding our old people mouthfuls of mush, we scrutinized the faces and eyes of the other seniors around us.

"Over there, that lady. She's wearing Susan's glasses, I'm sure of it," I told Cole and we flagged the cafeteria goth over to help us make the switch. Mystery solved, a success!

Johann ate through his entire pork schnitzel, too, at least that's what the menu posted on the bulletin board suggested the brown puddle was. A smaller success but still fulfilling. Detention aside, I felt pretty good about the day's events.

That Friday, after school in the car, I talked to Donovan about my volunteer work. "Yeah, yeah," he answered in two quick sound bites, a code that signalled the topic was too boring for him. Of course, he had to watch the road ahead of him, too, so he didn't make eye contact.

Then I told him about how I'd noticed that one lady had stolen the other's glasses.

"Yeah, yeah," he answered.

"First we went to the shower room to see if her glasses had been left there after her bath. But they weren't. And the attendant said she knew she'd put the silver-rimmed ones on her that morning."

"Yeah, yeah."

"Well, Gillian told us that they visit each other's rooms and sometimes steal from each other. Silly things, too. Family photos, combs, creams. In this case we figure she switched her eyeglasses."

"No kidding. What does the staff do when something valuable disappears?" He looked my way for a moment.

"I've never heard about anything like that happening," I answered. "They shouldn't have valuables lying around. Hey!" I gripped Donovan's arm. "Watch out for the woman with the stroller!"

He turned his attention to the road again and braked sharply. "But that lady you dyed the hair for — didn't she have money in her drawer?"

"I guess you're right."

"And the married ones, wouldn't they all have diamond rings? Do the families just take them away?"

"I don't know, Donny. What do you care?"

"I just wondered, that's all."

chapter nine

The next day the jury walks in dressed in the same array of jeans and sweatsuits as the day before. Kiwi lady wears a blueberry-coloured track suit with not so much as a tick-mark logo on it. The plaid-shirt man with the relaxed-fit jeans looks like he's wearing exactly the same clothes as before. Maybe he has a whole closet of red plaid shirts. I shouldn't judge. The lady with the stained top wears a clean one today. Could be it only stains during lunch.

The chubby guy wears a bright yellow golf shirt that screams, "Look at my potbelly." The other members of the jury look a bit rumpled, maybe a bit more tired.

As I take my place in the courtroom, I stare at the judge's shiny bald head. It bothers me for some reason, tugging at some image stuck somewhere in my head. Then it hits me — the dream about Omi.

Sitting in the courtroom now, I can hear her singing again in my head and my eyes fill up. She would help me if she could, wherever she was. Still, it doesn't matter if God counts me with his stars in the heavens or whether Omi loves me or not. It only matters what those twelve rumpled, tired jurors think as they listen to all the witnesses testifying.

"Would Donovan Petrocelli take the stand, please?"

Oh no, here it comes. I squeeze my eyes shut for a minute.

"Show me who your friends are and I'll tell you who you are," my mother said when I got caught shoplifting last summer. I had explained to her that I never stole anything. Donovan just passed a leather jacket to me to hold while he grabbed something else. The secret shopper pointed both of us out to the security guard and the two of them cornered us.

The charges were dropped for me but not for Donovan. Mom and Dad forbade me to see him. But, really, how could they stop me when they were busy working at the condo or were at tests and treatments for Mom?

Donovan's wearing a white shirt, dark tie, and a dark jacket. Dressed for court, or maybe a funeral. He affirms instead of swearing in on the Bible. You have that choice if you're not religious, but already it sets him apart from everyone else. His eyes, constantly moving, twitching almost, also set him apart. I don't know whether he still likes me or if he'll say bad things deliberately. But his eyes stop twitching as he sees me and he smiles.

"Donovan, under what circumstances did you meet Sonja Ehret, the defendant?"

"A couple of summers ago, I was working with a lawn-cutting company and we got hired by her old man's condo management company. One day I was mowing the lawn and she came out with a cold glass of water."

"How would you characterize your relationship?"

"Say what?"

"Were you just friends, or romantically involved . . ." the buzzard waves a hand windshield-wiper style, "you know, boyfriend, girlfriend."

"Yeah, yeah. I asked her out after I finished the glass of water. She goes to my high school and I'd seen her around before."

"So she would have been sixteen and you would have been seventeen, is that correct?"

Donovan shakes his head. "No, she was sixteen. I was nineteen."

The buzzard taps his chin. "A three-year age difference. Do you know whether or not her parents approved of your relationship?"

"They forbade her to see me."

"But you remained a couple for how long?"

"Um . . . um . . ." He glances at my parents, knowing that we were supposed to have broken up that August when the security guard called Mom in. "We stopped goin' out in February."

"That's seven months that Sonja had to sneak around and deceive her parents in order to see you."

"Objection!" my lawyer calls.

"Sustained," the judge answers.

Heh, heh, the plaid-shirt guy coughs. The chubby guy wipes his forehead hard and fast. Another statement they're not supposed to listen to and yet they react to it anyway.

"Can you tell the court why your relationship ended?"

"She got really involved with the old people at the home. It was supposed to be just to get her volunteer hours to graduate, but then it was all she ever talked about."

"Can you tell us some of the things she said to you about them?"

"Well, sure. You can see for yourself that Sunny is a hot . . . I mean, an attractive girl. She wanted them all to look

76

better — to wear nicer clothes, to have their hair styled. We used to shop for them. She wanted to make them all happier and better."

"How did she react when instead the seniors slipped further away?"

"She was really bummed out. She said she'd rather die than live the way they did."

"Objection!" my lawyer calls.

"Overruled," the judge says. "This is not hearsay. Mr. Petrocelli actually heard these words himself."

That's because I must have said that line a hundred times to him before I even met Helen Demers, like when we were just shopping in the mall on Senior's Day. Lining up behind the old folks as they stuttered forward on their canes or walkers, watching runny eyes trying to read the fine print on a coupon or shaky fingers groping for change in a clutch purse, or hearing clerks call the seniors "Dear" as they returned the change.

"Just shoot me," Donovan would agree as a scooter driven by an old guy on oxygen rolled along beside us.

But I've changed! Now, every time I see one of those elderly people struggling with their shopping, I want to call out "Good for you! Good you can still do it. You're a hundred times better off than those old people back in Paradise Manor."

"Donovan, in front of you is a record of crimes you have committed. Do you acknowledge these?"

"Yes sir."

"You agree this a true representation of your crimes."

"Yeah, but Sunny had nothing to do with these."

Don't do me any favours, Donny.

"Ladies and gentlemen of the jury, you have before you Donovan Petrocelli's criminal record, which shows several convictions for shoplifting. No further questions."

Donovan meant well, but he did harm. I can tell by the way the guy with the yellow shirt folds his arms. "Show me your friends . . ." my mother had said. That guy thought he knew who I was from the boyfriend I used to have. What that whole jury didn't understand was that I grew out of Donovan and a lot of the feelings I used to have. And I really put a lot of myself into my work at Paradise Manor. They just had to check my journal.

The Ninth Visit — twenty-two hours left

Mrs. Johnson may tell you I broke the rules again, Mr. Brooks, but I have to tell you I feel really good about my volunteer work today. I spent some time alone with Johann Schwartz and I was able to feed him his entire meal after he'd had a very rough morning.

For the first snowfall of the season, I sure didn't ride my bike to Paradise Manor. From my seat by the window of the bus I spotted Cole, though, riding his. He wore a blue toque under his red helmet. I shook my head. What his hair would look like after that!

I'd actually borrowed some of Donovan's hair glue, permanently, and kept it in my purse especially for Cole. When we walked into the home together, after sterilizing our hands, I gelled down his hair. I could smell his breath as I used my own comb to place the strands of his hair just so. Wintergreen, much nicer than mint.

He drew closer but then pulled away. "You have a boyfriend, don't you, Sunny."

It was a statement and a discouraged one at that. I smiled at him. "We're not engaged to be married."

He smiled back.

"We are supposed to go to his graduation prom together."

He pursed his lips. "Kind of like temporarily married."

I shrugged my shoulders. "We'll see."

We headed over to the door of the lockup unit and he keyed in the code. Right from the doorway, I heard someone crying. A man.

"Who's that?" Cole wondered out loud.

"Let's check." We walked quickly, bypassing all the stone-faced wheelchair gnomes lining the walls. Past Susan rocking her baby, past Fred and Marlene shopping for bread or auto parts. A wide band of yellow tape stretched across the door from frame to frame, blocking off Johann Schwartz's room as though it were a crime scene or something.

"He's by himself for his own protection," Sheila, the cafeteria goth, told us as she pushed a cart with trays of covered dishes through the hall.

"What do you mean? I'm supposed to feed him. He can't do it by himself."

"He's been yelling too much. He upset the others. He can't eat in the dining room."

"I can still feed him though. I'll do it in his room if he bothers the others."

Sheila shook her head. "It's absolutely against the rules. We can't be responsible for you all alone with him."

Blah, blah, blah. I could hear her talking, but Johann's crying blocked me from really processing it. I stared at the yellow tape.

"It's meant to keep the others from going in there," Sheila explained. "For his own safety. The tape is enough to stop the others."

"But not me." I couldn't help myself. I yanked the yellow barrier down and walked into the room.

In the far corner Johann sat, blue eyes swimming, his left cheek bright red but turning blue near the eye.

"You can't be with him by yourself." Gillian suddenly rushed into the room from behind me.

"But he's crying." I looked back at her. "Why does he have to be by himself?"

"Jeannette hit him when he wouldn't stop yelling."

"Why doesn't Jeannette sit alone then?"

"Last time it was Susan."

"Susan hit him?"

Gillian shrugged her shoulders. "He made her baby cry."

Johann sobbed.

"But now he's crying. I'll get him to stop. Then I'll feed him."

She shook her head. "Mrs. Johnson won't like it."

"Then sit down beside me and watch." I wasn't leaving.

She sighed. "We'll keep the door open and check on you now and again. Sheila, bring the food in."

Cole doubled back to look after his grandmother, but Sheila and Gillian took their time leaving. I didn't wait. I took some tissue from the box in the bathroom and carefully dried the tears from Johann's face. Then I sang to him in my crummy voice that Jeannette thought was so beautiful. I sang softly in German the lullaby that my grandmother used to sing to me. "*Weist Du wiefiel Sternlien stehen am dem blauen Himmelzelt.*" The song about how God looks after the stars and loves us too.

It was the only German song I knew. The lullaby used to comfort me. When Johann settled down, I fed him the plops of different-coloured mush on his plate before he fell asleep.

When I finally joined Cole and his grandmother, they were having tea in chairs near the courtyard window. Outside a sole snowflake drifted down. Then another and another, more quickly, until it was as if someone had shaken a feather pillow.

Jeannette stopped by to tell me how beautiful my smile was. My mouth was gripped tightly so that I wouldn't tell her off about hitting Johann. She shuffled on.

"It's not her fault," Cole said as he took my hand.

"She understands better than most of them," I grumbled.

"Who knows what part of her brain is broken. Which section is covered in plaque. She's in the lockup for a reason and not just because she doesn't know a pair of jeans from a skirt."

Not her fault. Not in her right mind. Not herself.

Just like what he said about his mom when she blew up over Helen's hair colouring. I forgave Jeannette, just like I forgave Claudine Demers then, too.

As I stare across the courtroom, I'm having a much harder time forgiving her today.

chapter ten

My lawyer decides he wants to question Donovan, and I switch my attention back to the witness stand.

"You said you met Sonja two summers ago while mowing the lawn. Can you tell us how she acted towards you?"

"Sorry. I'm not sure what you mean."

"Did she laugh a lot, flirt maybe?"

"No, she was very quiet. If anything she acted bored mostly. There wasn't anything for her to do at the condo office. She was supposed to be helping out, answering the phone and opening the mail 'cause her mom was recovering from surgery."

"How did Sunny react to her mother being treated for cancer?"

"I dunno. I thought she was just angry about spending her summer at the condo office. But it was more than that. Like she was just angry at her mother about something else."

"When you met her, did she have pink streaks in her hair?"

"Not right away. That's something she did after we went out."

"Do you think she would have gone out with you if her mother didn't have cancer?"

"Objection!" the buzzard calls out.

"Sustained," the judge answers.

Michael smiles. He's made his point anyway. Maybe I snuck around behind my parents' backs to go out with a shoplifter, as the Crown showed, but I only did it because my mother's illness put me in a crazy state of mind. "No further questions."

The Tenth Visit — twenty hours left

I missed feeding Johann today. They shipped him off to St. Peter's Hospital where they have more staff so they can adjust his medication and get him to stop yelling. Instead I sat with Fred and Marlene and three other residents. I fed two at a time. I'm getting good at this, Mr. Brooks.

What I didn't tell him in that journal entry is how it felt when I arrived ahead of Cole and hunted for Johann all by myself. It's not easy to spot a specific inmate when you're looking for him because most of them have grey hair, sleep a lot, and slump forward in their wheelchairs as they snooze. I walked the circuit twice, stopping in the recreation room. No ranting or crying in German or otherwise. Then, I remembered, they probably still had him locked behind yellow tape. I rushed past Jeannette.

"Hello, Gorgeous," she called after me.

At Johann's room, the door was open. The bed had been stripped as though no one lived there anymore. Was he dead?

"Good riddance."

I jumped. Jeannette's voice came from just behind me. When I turned around, there she stood with her bright lip-sticked grin. "The old fool went on a trip."

"What kind of trip?"

She shrugged her shoulders, her grin a smirk now.

I rushed to the nursing station but couldn't find anyone. I caught a cleaner by her sleeve and asked about Johann. She told me to talk to Gillian.

"But I don't see her anywhere either!"

"Check the front desk."

Gillian wasn't there, but the hand sanitizing commando, Katherine, had returned to her post. That's how I found out about Johann's "trip." And I might have been relieved, but by the tone of Katherine's voice, I knew this was not a good thing.

"Is he ever coming back?" I asked her.

"I hope so. Not many people do."

Cole came in then. When I told him what had happened, he just hugged me. Together we headed for the dining room and helped our old people eat. Marlene kissed Fred and he kissed her back.

"Aren't we lucky," she told him.

"Are you Diane?" he returned.

She ignored his question as he did hers. Instead she continued to repeat how lucky they were.

He continued to wonder out loud when Diane would come.

Finally Jeannette told them to shut up or she would take them both out.

Leaving Paradise Manor that day certainly made me feel lucky.

That evening I asked Wolfie for help with my Remembrance Day project.

"Remembrance Day, seriously?" Wolfie shook his head.

"Sunny, that was three weeks ago!"

"I'm a little late." More like a month. "But I had trouble with it. I don't like 'remembering' war."

"Well, it doesn't get any easier if you drag it out. You're a smart girl. Figure out what you have to do to get your marks."

"I did! And Mr. Brooks understands. I told him I wanted to forget about war. And I wanted to talk about losing remembrance instead. He gave me an extension."

Wolfie raised an eyebrow. "So what kind of help do you need?"

I took out my phone. "I want to download these photos and put them in a slideshow." I showed him the research I'd done and told him my idea. Together we figured out how to put it together and then I practiced in front of him.

"Sunny, you're so creative. Are you sure you want to become a hairdresser?"

"You know I've loved playing with hair since I was little. I can be creative with styling."

"Well, once you have all the education and training you need, I'll partner with you to buy your own salon." That was high praise from my brother. He knows everything about making good investments.

The next day I stood in front of the class, a large screen behind me. I felt pretty confident presenting my version of a Remembrance project. "Alzheimer's is a disease affecting one in eight people over age sixty-five. On the left you see a normal brain, on the right is one affected by Alzheimer's." I used my laser pointer to show the pockets of plaque.

"Gross," Shane called out. "That must be what Jordan has."

"See me after class," Mr. Brooks snapped.

I smiled and continued.

"People used to accept forgetfulness and dementia as a normal symptom of aging." The next slide was a picture of an older man with a brush cut, moustache, and glasses attached to a string.

"That was until Alois Alzheimer came along and examined the brain of a fifty-one-year-old woman who had exhibited strange behaviour and died in his insane asylum. He discovered this plaque.

"If I were Alois, I sure wouldn't want to have a brain-destroying illness named after me because I was the person to discover it," I commented.

Julie and Lena snickered over this one.

"Me neither," Jordan called out.

"Class!" Mr. Brooks warned from his seat in the back. They quieted down immediately. "You're off track, Sunny," Mr. Brooks told me.

"Sorry." I flipped back to the previous slide with the brains. "Because the plaques destroy nerve cells, the patient loses memory and cognitive reasoning. They can't think. Then eventually they can't read, walk, go to the bathroom by themselves, eat, swallow . . . or breathe. And they die.

"But it can take a long time. Seven to fourteen years before they finally forget how to live." I flipped ahead again. "Here are some photos of the people I've worked with at Paradise Manor."

I showed them Fred, Marlene, Johann, Jeannette, and Cole's grandma, and told them what they had been and the things they did now.

"Wow, that must drive you crazy," Julie commented.

"No. But it is hard as a volunteer to even know how best

to help them sometimes. You want to humour them, but then they get confused and anxious about whatever you've said or done to go along with them. Fred looked like he was going to cry when I gave him the old shifter from my Dad's Mustang. Jeannette nearly hit me when I suggested she had to make new friends. Sometimes the patients cry, go into rages, laugh on and on, or yell. Or they just sit and sleep.

"I think the hardest thing about the disease is the effect it has on the family. I mean the person herself is . . . like almost comatose. How much could it bother her at that point? But I've seen other people visit their relatives in the home and even I just find it hard to deal with the shell that the victim becomes.

"I used to be afraid of cancer. My grandmother died of it at the age of fifty-six and my mother is in remission since last summer.

"Now I'm way more afraid of Alzheimer's Disease. I'd rather die of cancer.

"In conclusion, I would like to say that researchers are working on vaccines and pills that carry antibodies for Alzheimer's. It just takes a long time to see if the medicines work. And while we're waiting, brain cells die just like that." I snapped my fingers. "Imaginative and intelligent people turn into zombies." The last slides showed famous people who died of Alzheimer's. "Movie stars Rita Hayworth, Charles Bronson, and Charlton Heston; boxer Sugar Ray Robinson; singer Perry Como; famous British dude from World War II, Winston Churchill —"

"Wait a minute . . ." Mr. Brooks interrupted, "Winston Churchill had Alzheimer's?"

"Some people say that. Others argue that it was a different version of dementia. And the fortieth American president,

Ronald Reagan." I paused to look around the room and make eye contact one final time. "Thank you for listening to my presentation on Alzheimer's."

Everyone clapped politely, the way we were taught.

"Thank you, Sunny," Mr. Brooks said when the applause ended. "Good work. Any questions or comments?"

Lena asked if there was any way to prevent people from getting the disease.

"I don't believe there is. You're supposed to exercise and keep your blood pressure and weight down. But that's the doctors' answers to everything. Just like washing your hands."

"What about blueberries? I heard eating them improves your memory," Julie asked.

"Vitamin E," Brittany called.

"Fish is brain food," Jordan argued.

"You're supposed to do puzzles, like crosswords or Sudoku," Shawna said. "My grandfather likes word searches."

I shrugged my shoulders. "Nobody really knows yet. And there are some really smart people in Paradise Manor. I mean they used to be smart. I don't think they chowed down on junk food or anything."

"I heard that if we don't find the cure, baby boomers will bankrupt the healthcare system as they get Alzheimer's."

"What do you think about that, Sunny?" Mr. Brooks asked me.

"I don't know. But scientists are curing all the diseases that used to kill us before getting to the point where our brains started rotting. Maybe we'll have to decide when to put people to sleep. The residents I volunteer with sleep most of the time anyway. We do it for our pets. We decide they're suffering too much and put them out of their misery."

"But Sunny, aren't these seniors well looked after? Are they really suffering?" Mr. Brooks asked.

"They've lost their memories and the lives they used to know. They're mixed up, sad, and anxious sometimes. Yes, I think they're suffering a lot."

Mr. Brooks gave me an A+ on this presentation. I felt sure I was almost home free on the volunteer requirement and journal. When I was charged, though, the principal decided my forty hours at the residence couldn't be counted. Or my journal either. Unless I was acquitted.

chapter eleven

"The crown calls Alexis Meredith to the stand."

Alexis is my best friend, despite everything that's happened. She's stuck with me throughout this whole year no matter what the other kids said. My lawyer said if she hadn't agreed to testify for the Crown, they would have subpoenaed her anyway. Still, what can the buzzard ask her that will make me seem in the wrong?

She states her name and swears on the Bible. Alexis keeps her hair its natural golden colour. She wears a minimal amount of makeup: a clear lip balm and mascara only because her eyelashes would otherwise appear white. But her eyes are large and blue and she's wearing a navy blue V-necked sweater over a white shirt paired with navy slacks. The sweater looks soft, angora maybe? Anyhow, the total effect is that Lexie looks angelic. The jury's going to like her.

The buzzard starts. "Miss Meredith, what's your relationship to Sonja Ehret?"

"She's my best friend."

"And what kind of things do you do together?"

"Oh, you know, hang out, play Wii games, Guitar Hero . . . We shop."

"She invited you to Paradise Manor, did she not?"

"Yes, one time when we decorated trees for a raffle. Sunny is always good with that kind of thing."

Only one time. Yes, I had been small-minded about keeping her away from Cole. I didn't invite her back for the party.

"How did you find Sunny treated the residents?"

"She was really nice to them. She humoured them, you know?"

"Would you say she would do anything they asked?"

"Objection! Leading," my lawyer shouts.

"Sustained," the judge answers.

"What about Cole? Were you able to form an opinion on how he treated his grandma?"

"He was really kind to all the seniors. Gentle with his grandma."

"Can you tell us of any specific behaviours?"

"Sure. He helped her put on a sweater. Got her another cup of tea when she spilled the first one. Held her hand."

"Did he give her things to eat?"

Alexis stays quiet. Her lips purse.

Heh, heh, the plaid-shirted guy coughs.

"Miss Meredith?"

"Just as he left he gave her a candy."

"Was it a hard candy?"

Alexis hesitates again. The jury members get restless, scratching, forehead scrubbing, and coughing.

Come on, Lexie, answer already. She was calling too much attention to the stupid question.

"I couldn't say for sure, but it looked like it came from a bag of Werther's Originals."

"No further questions."

Oh, come on. It shouldn't be about what Cole gave his grandma. The trial should be about what I did.

The Eleventh Visit — eighteen hours left

Besides feeding the old folk, today I helped decorate the common areas for Christmas. Even Mrs. Johnson admired my work. She asked me and the other volunteer, Cole, to come back on the weekend to decorate the small trees they raffle off as prizes. So if you're not counting the first visit cancelled due to smell, let's count that extra Saturday visit. And by the way, do you want to buy a ticket, Mr. Brooks? You could use the tree in the classroom. Frankly, it's a bit drab in there. They'll be raffled off next week at the party.

"Tell me why you're not going Christmas shopping with me again?" Donovan asked on the phone when I said I had volunteer duties on Saturday.

As we talked, I tucked the phone in my shoulder and started picking up lint from the Berber carpet in my bedroom. "It's a fundraiser for Paradise Manor. You can come help too. Alexis is." I forced myself to sound hopeful. My room is painted a chirpy canary yellow and I find focusing on bright colours always helps.

But really, I counted on Donovan not volunteering with us. I thought he'd make fun of the old people. Also I didn't know how I'd feel with him and Cole in the same room. Donovan was way hotter, there was no doubt about that, but Cole was considerate and kind. I really didn't want him shown up.

There was another nagging feeling tugging at me. Cole's

personality might just totally show Donovan up. I still had my heart set on attending his graduation prom. It would be practice for my own. Nothing's quite as big as a grad dance, unless maybe it's your wedding. I pitched the lint from my hand into the wastepaper basket and straightened.

"You're going to want me to steal presents for the old folks soon. We could have started today," Donovan told me.

"I don't want you to steal anything." My duvet looked annoyingly wrinkled so I straightened and smoothed it. "Get another job, Donny. The stores are all looking for help." Of course, with his shoplifting conviction, maybe no one would hire him.

"But it's the challenge, Sunny. Nothing gives me quite the rush. I try to pay sometimes and this feeling just comes over me . . . and I can't help myself."

"Well, go enjoy then." I punched hard at the pillows on my bed to plump them up.

"Let me take you for lunch first and I'll drive you to the home after."

I stared at the sunshine of my walls and breathed in deeply. "Alexis is coming too, remember?"

"So I'll swing round and pick her up too."

Another inhale of the brightness. "Sure, that sounds great." Donny did have his good points. He could be very generous. We agreed that I would be ready for eleven and then we hung up.

That Saturday he ended up taking me and Alexis to lunch and he even paid. I squirmed in my seat when he honked at the red bicycle ahead of us turning onto the Manor drive.

"What kind of idiot drives a bike in winter?" he said.

"Someone who wants to stay fit and cares for the

environment," Alexis answered. "Is that the guy you were telling me about, Sunny?"

Donovan drove us to the front door where Cole was locking up his bike. I don't know if he saw or not, but Donny picked then to give me the slowest kiss of the decade. Alexis had jumped out of the car and introduced herself to Cole by the time it ended.

Alexis is a lot taller than me and thin like Cole. Her hair curls around her face like a lion's mane and her eyes make her stand out in a girl-next-door kind of way. Plus she's smart, way smarter than me. Standing with Cole chatting, she looked like she belonged with him and that made something crack open inside of me. Something I didn't even know was there.

Donovan gave a double honk on his horn and I waved goodbye without looking back. "Hey, Cole," I called. Even though his hair stuck up rooster style as usual, I didn't feel comfortable fixing it for him in front of Alexis.

"Hi, Sunny," he answered back stiff and uncomfortable, as though I'd interrupted something. Or was it Donovan's kiss that was bothering him?

We went inside. Alexis loved the jaunty bow and cap I'd given the ceramic bulldog in the foyer. "That fireplace could use some stockings hung in a row, though."

I shrugged. "We worked with what we had."

"Maybe I can get a store to donate some," Alexis said. "I got sponsors to give us dog treats for the shelter."

I thought about the sweatpants Donovan had stolen for Fred and Johann. You could say we had forced a store into sponsorship.

We headed into the crafts room on the second floor. Some silver-haired ladies there were crocheting slippers for a bazaar that would be held the day before the party. Gillian walked around, chatting with them.

There were ten trees spread along the counters that lined the wall and plastic bags of brand-new decorations on the table across from the crocheters. A boom box in the corner played Christmas music. At that moment, one of Dad's crooners, Bing Crosby I think, was singing "White Christmas."

One of the ladies sang along, another hummed.

Cole broke into song as he ripped open a bag of little pink-and-gold angels playing trumpets and harps.

Alexis smiled an admiring yet sympathetic kind of smirk.

I don't know what got into me, but I sang, too, as I attached tiny red-velvet bows to a tree.

Alexis hung golden bells on her tree. When "White Christmas" ended, the "The Little Drummer Boy" began. Alexis started singing that one in her best crystal tones. One of the crocheting ladies told her she had a lovely voice. These women didn't live in the lockup unit. It didn't seem like they had any form of dementia. I missed Jeannette's compliments.

"Don't hang that." I yanked down a silver ball from Cole's angel-covered tree.

"Why not?" he asked.

"You have enough on already. And you don't want to mix silver with gold. No one will buy tickets for it."

"Christmas is all about too much," Alexis said. "Anything goes." To bug me she added a silver ball to her tree.

But I thought she was wrong. Christmas is about beautiful things: my grandmother's advent candles sitting on an evergreen wreath, the scent of burnt candles and pine needles, an elegant table set with linen, crystal glasses, and bone-coloured dishes. My mother, in a silk dress, well and smiling over it all.

"Don't use too many decorations on one tree," Gillian warned. "Or we'll run out."

"Yeah, Alexis." I yanked off the silver ball.

When we were finished all the trees looked good, even the garish Snoopy tree Cole did. We wrapped small, empty tissue boxes to hold the ballot tickets.

Afterwards we went into the lockup to see Mrs. Demers. We drank apple juice and ate ornament-shaped sugar cookies at the window overlooking the courtyard. Of course, Cole's grandma just had a plain tea biscuit. She didn't say anything but her eyes looked warmly at Cole. Whether she recognized him or not, she loved him.

"Where did you get those? I never got anything to eat and I'm starving," Marlene complained as she shuffled by with Fred.

"Here, have mine," I held out my plate.

She took it and ate the cookie standing up.

"Are you Diane?" Fred asked me.

"No. Sunny."

"No it's not. It's snowing outside," Marlene said. She finished the cookie and pointed to Cole's. "Where did you get that? They never gave me any and I'm starving."

By the time we left, Marlene had eaten six cookies and was still starving. She also needed a loaf of bread and Fred wanted us to take him to Canadian Tire.

As Cole kissed his grandma goodbye, he unwrapped a butterscotch candy and slipped it into her mouth.

"Thank you," she mumbled around it, the candy clicking against her teeth. They were her only words that afternoon.

"I love you, Grandma. No matter what."

"Bye Helen. Bye Fred. Bye Marlene." Alexis waved to everyone.

Someone grabbed my arm. When I turned, I saw it was Jeannette. "Those are beautiful shoes you have on." Jeannette didn't even glance Alexis's way. At least she was loyal.

"Thank you." I was wearing lace-up leather boots up to my knees. Still, her oddball comment made me feel appreciated. In that one small way, she reminded me of my grandmother. "See you at the Christmas party."

"Merry Christmas," she said and shuffled off.

Cole didn't want to join us at the mall no matter how Alexis coaxed him.

"Gawd, could you make yourself any more desperate?" I said in frustration as we boarded the bus.

"What are you talking about?" she asked, picking the first double seat at the front.

"You. Chasing Cole. He obviously didn't want to come shopping with us and you kept at him." I slid in beside her.

She clicked her tongue and rolled her eyes, then stared out the window.

"And the whole time you flirted with him."

She turned towards me. "So? What's wrong with that? I'm not going out with anyone."

"Doesn't mean you have to smother a guy."

"You have Donovan." She raised her voice and sputtered, "You said you don't even like Cole. Why can't I have him? Is there one boy on earth you don't have to have?"

Sitting on the long seat just ahead of us, a lady with a fun-fur Cossack hat turned around to stare.

I lowered my voice. She faced the front again. "I can't help it if Cole likes me."

"Sunny, he finds you pretty. All boys do." Her voice rose and the Cossack hat flipped around again. "'Cause you are!

You are beautiful." She noogied the side of my head. "Get that through your skull!"

"Watch the hair!" I pulled my head away. "You know what? I really don't feel like shopping after all." I stood up, yanked the signal bell and walked to the front of the bus.

"Sunny, come back!"

But I couldn't. Because even though I still wanted to go out with Donovan, I knew then that I also wanted to keep Cole all to myself. Maybe if I had just been honest about how I felt about Cole instead of taking it out on Alexis, I wouldn't be in this courtroom today.

chapter twelve

"Alexis, you stated before that Sonja Ehret was your best friend. What qualities did you see in her to form such a relationship?"

"Well, we live in the same neighbourhood and have been in the same class since about kindergarten."

"Go on."

"We enjoy the same things — fashion, boys." My lawyer nods and she continues. "But what I really like about Sunny is that she's kind and generous. She's really sensitive, too, but she covers that up. She always tries to be cheery."

"Is that where she got her nickname?"

"Yeah. Her family calls her that so of course her friends do."

"Can you give us an example of her sensitivity?"

"Well, when her mom got sick I knew she was really down about it even though most people didn't see it. So I suggested we sign up for Run for the Cure."

"And she agreed."

"Yes, and she hates jogging. But then when she had to get pledges, she found she couldn't talk about it. So we didn't run. That's when she streaked her hair pink."

"So you're saying she colours her hair to increase awareness of breast cancer?"

"Yeah, but she still can't really talk about it, so I don't know if that's exactly working out."

"Would you say Sonja is the kind of person who likes to take charge, or is she more of a follower?"

Alexis thinks this question over. She is my best friend and she wants to answer what's right for me, I know it. But her hesitation makes her seem unsure. "Sunny is a leader."

I know what my lawyer wanted from that question. Just because Cole made a promise to his grandmother, it didn't mean I would follow his plan. Would they draw the right conclusion though? I look at the jury. Nobody seems to be dozing off today. Or will they just think *Sunny didn't just assist with a suicide because of a boy she loved. Sunny led the way.*

The Twelfth Visit — sixteen hours left

At the Christmas party tons of people came and there was lots of food. My job was to get residents with no family their refreshments. That was Johann and Marlene. That's right, Mr. Brooks, Johann came back. Fred's wife attended the party so I really felt bad for Marlene. Also, sorry to say, you didn't win a tree.

No one told me Johann was returning but when I arrived at Paradise Manor, an ambulance was parked in front. As I passed through the two sets of doors, I saw a small reception crew fussing: Katherine and Gillian, Mrs. Johnson and a new male nurse I didn't know. In the middle I could make out Johann sitting in a wheelchair.

"You came back just in time. Santa Claus is coming today, Papa," the nurse told him.

"We're so happy you're home," Katherine said. I liked her

better because she really sounded as though she meant it.

I rushed over. "*Frohe Weihnachten!*" I told him. "Merry Christmas" in German. Then I hugged him and kissed his cheek, which was warm but stiff. He needed a good moisturizer.

I looked in his eyes. The pupils were as small as needle points and he didn't even blink. He no longer ranted. He seemed somewhere else but here in this chair sat his body as a place mark.

I frowned, feeling like I'd lost something, too.

As they wheeled him back to his room to get him ready for the party, I joined Cole in the dining room. A Santa Claus who looked familiar was setting up a speaker system.

"Elvis is back," Cole told me, waggling his eyebrows.

On the right side of the room a banquet table held festive-looking food: a shrimp tree, meatballs in a crockpot, crustless sandwiches on green and pink bread, multi-grain rolls and roses of butter, sausages in puff pastry, and squares and cookies of every flavour and shape.

The regular tables were crowded with residents and their families. I saw the pirate boy from Halloween with some kind of red punch staining the corners of his mouth: Boo Berry juice turned Christmas Cranberry. He carried a plateful of meatballs over to a table where his grandmother sat. She was one of the seniors I still didn't know.

By another table, I saw Fred being kissed by a leopard-print-wearing blonde. Hussy! Although the lady probably was his real wife. Still, how was Marlene going to take this? She sat at the corner of a table with Susan. Luckily, Cole's grandmother was parked there too, so Cole and I could work together.

"Merry Christmas, Marlene!" I said. I strolled over to the

table to load up a plate with two rolls and some meatballs and gravy. "Here you go. Look Marlene, see all the nice bread. You won't have to go to the store today."

That made her turn her head towards Fred's table. She always walked the halls with Fred to shop for her imaginary bread. She gave him a wave once or twice but he didn't even look her way.

"Do you like shrimp? I can get you some."

She didn't answer. Instead she picked up her fork and continued to watch Fred and his leopard-spotted wife. She was feeding him shrimp. I saw a handsome man maybe my father's age who looked just like Fred. His son. You could see what Fred must have been like when he was healthier.

At that moment, Gillian wheeled Johann in and parked him right by Marlene.

I got him some sausages. I thought they might be soft enough for him.

Marlene put her hand on his.

There you go Marlene, there are more fish in the sea. Santa Elvis began to sing. "I'll have a bluh, bluh blue Christmas without you."

I looked around. Maybe it wasn't exactly a blue Christmas at Paradise Manor. There were lots of people dressed in Santa hats and bright colours trying to seem festive, pretending everyone was having fun.

"Merry Christmas!" Gillian gurgled, her Rudolph brooch flashing red at its nose. Was she really this enthusiastic? Most of the residents responded the same as they always did, which was not at all. They just stared off, slack-jawed, mumbling, or even snoring. Only Jeannette smiled, her head swaying in time to the music. Of course at any minute, if she had a mood switch, she might threaten to kill Santa.

I cut up the little sausage rolls for Johann and put one in his mouth. He began coughing immediately. I watched his colour and waited. Meanwhile I buttered Marlene's roll. Cole winked at me as he slipped his grandmother a toffee square from the desert table. Yeah, like that was dietetic.

"Do you want a drink, Johann?"

He coughed some more. *Hek, hek, hek, hek.*

I held a glass of the red punch to his lips and he drank some. At least I saw his Adam's apple bob a few times as though he were swallowing. But some of the red stained his face just like it had the young pirate.

"Better to let him catch his breath on his own. Don't give him anything to drink till he does," Gillian told me as she drifted closer. "Are you okay, Johann?"

He ignored her and continued his little coughs. Gradually they slowed down. I got him some trifle, which was more custard then cake, and he did much better on that.

Santa Elvis sang that he would be home for Christmas, then he revisited some more traditional tunes — "O Little Town of Bethlehem," "O Come All Ye Faithful," "Silent Night." One song after another. Between sets, Christmas-tree raffle winners were announced over the intercom. Cole won the Snoopy tree he had decorated.

"You bought a ticket for your own tree?" I asked.

"Five actually for each of mine. I was worried everyone else would buy tickets only for the ones you decorated."

I shook my head at him and smiled. "Silly."

Finally most of the food was gone and one by one the residents were by themselves. When the leopard lady and her family left, I took Marlene by the hand and brought her back to Fred.

He asked me if I was Diane.

"Wasn't Diane just here?" I asked, thinking the younger woman at the table might have been his daughter.

"Darn. I forgot to ask her. I need to find my car. I don't know where I left it. It needs a part."

"Well, do you want to go for a walk with Marlene?" I asked, but he stood before I finished the sentence and took her hand.

You don't have to forgive when you have Alzheimer's, because you always forget. Marlene acted as though they had never been apart. Away they went.

That left Cole and me alone with two catatonic seniors. "Wasn't that a great party, Grandma?" he said.

She didn't answer, but she smiled.

"Are you happy to be home, Johann?" I asked my senior.

Nothing. No response, not even an eye blinked. Was this better than having him yell all the time? I wasn't certain.

It was time to go. Cole and I said our goodbyes and he removed a sparkly gold wrapper from a candy and slipped it into his grandmother's mouth. We didn't wait to see if she chewed or sucked at it. No big deal, we just left.

On the way out, Cole picked up his prize. "Here, I want you to have this. Merry Christmas."

"Thank you." I took the Snoopy-covered little fir and then reached over it to kiss him. It was supposed to just be a friendly peck. But somehow my lips landed directly on his and stayed there. The spiced candy cane mint kiss tingled on my lips long after I pulled away. That kiss should have told Cole how I felt, even if I never got the chance to.

chapter thirteen

The next witness for the Crown is Claudine Demers, Cole's mother. This shouldn't be a shock to me. My lawyer has a list of all the people the prosecution will use on the stand, and Cole's mother is on it.

Still, I've never met her and there she stands, Cole's mouth and eyes set in an older person's face. The wrinkles around them and the set of her face seem like a reaction to an ache. She uses the Bible to swear in. Good that she believes in God. That must have been helpful last year at this time.

The Crown attorney smoothes his black feathers and asks her to explain her relationship to the victim.

"I'm her daughter-in-law, but I also had power of attorney for finances and personal care."

He lifts his beak hopefully. "Isn't this unusual? Shouldn't it be her son, your husband, who holds this power?"

Claudine's mouth purses with a long-suffering air. "My husband travels for his work. Since I was the person most easily reached and available, Helen signed the papers over to me. We were quite close."

The buzzard nods. He's so understanding and he talks

more softly now. "How long has your mother-in-law had Alzheimer's disease?"

She frowns and shrugs her shoulders. "We don't know for sure. She may have been having symptoms before but she was diagnosed by a gerontologist four years ago."

"And what was the prognosis for the disease in her case?"

"The doctor had no predictions to make. We were just supposed to take it day by day. We did think that if she lived with us and we could administer the medications, it might slow the progression."

"And were you right?"

Mrs. Demers frowns and shakes her head. "No. Or, well, maybe it did. Still her condition deteriorated rapidly. She started accusing me of stealing things from her. She also went for long walks and got lost all the time."

The buzzard shifts on his feet and raises his palm up to her. "So she lived in your home for as long as possible and then you placed her in Paradise Manor?"

"It was after a car hit her." She stops abruptly.

Two bad accidents to people she loved. I feel a twinge for her again.

She continues. "We felt we had no other choice."

The Crown attorney tilts his head, his hand still reaching out. "How would you characterize your son's relationship with your mother-in-law?"

"Even though Helen stopped trusting me, and blamed me for forcing her into the home, she still believed in Cole. They had a strong bond." Claudine nods emphatically.

"Do you feel she might have asked him to assist her to commit suicide?"

"Absolutely."

The jury lady in the sweatsuit gasps.

Cole's mom quickly continues. "But that doesn't matter. Cole understood that the request was from a woman who no longer had her reasoning. He knew it to be wrong. He would not have helped her."

"You've never met Sonja Ehret before this trial, but from what he said at home, how would you characterize Cole's relationship to the defendant?"

Mrs. Demers frowns. "He liked her very much." She sounds sour about this as she continues. "He wanted her to be his girlfriend. On Valentine's Day he had a whole romantic evening planned with her for after their visit to the Manor. He even had his hair styled for the day."

The buzzard furrows his brow, pretending to be puzzled on the behalf of all of us. "Instead Cole just rode his bike away from the Paradise Manor that day?"

"I don't know what happened exactly. But I'm convinced she broke his heart."

Objection! Misunderstanding! I wanted to go out with Cole that night.

But I can't yell that out and, anyway, I'm not on trial for standing him up on a Valentine's date. Still, the round juror shifts uncomfortably in his chair. You can tell he's not happy with me. He's frowning and wiping his forehead.

"Do you feel your son might have extracted some promise from Sonja that she would help him in assisting your mother-in-law's suicide?"

"Objection!" My lawyer leaps up. "Opinions and hearsay."

"Sustained," the judge says.

"No, no, no!" Mrs. Demers cries out. "Cole wouldn't do that!"

"Mrs. Demers, you are not to answer that question. The objection was sustained," the judge warns.

"But it's wrong! Cole wouldn't dye Helen's hair pink, either. My mother-in-law had no mind anymore. But that girl," she pointed at me, "would have done anything she asked."

"Objection!"

"Sustained."

"No further questions."

She hates me, she hates me. There are no do-overs in her regard. But she doesn't know me. She should read my journal. She would know then that I never intended anyone any harm.

The Thirteenth Visit — fourteen hours left

Johann Schwartz died Wednesday, a week and a half before Christmas. Miss Halliday called and asked me to come on Friday for his "life celebration." She wanted the chapel to look full for the family. This was my second funeral ever, Mr. Brooks. I helped wheel some of the seniors in, so this definitely counts towards my hours. I hate funerals.

Cole's number was easy to find on Canada 411 so I called him. He sounded thrilled to hear my voice and I felt bad giving him the news. He didn't say a word. "So can you come with me? I'm really nervous that it might be open coffin. My grandma was in a closed one at the front of the room and I couldn't sleep with the light off for a year after. I don't think I can handle this without you."

"I'm already going. Gillian called me too."

"Oh, good. Where do you live? I'll get my brother Wolfie to drive us."

"Okay. Do you want to take down my address?"

I wrote it down and Wolfie programmed it into our GPS Friday morning. Cole lived in an older part of town with largish houses and big backyards.

When we rolled up, he was standing outside on the driveway dressed in a suit with a grey coat, unbuttoned, overtop. His hair was slicked back and he carried a red rose. He looked cute in an over-the-top, Sunday-best way.

"Shoot, were we supposed to bring flowers?" I asked when he reached for the car door.

"No, Sunny. I brought this one for you." He handed it to me. "You knew Johann only four months but you made a connection. I thought the rose might make you feel a little better."

I closed my eyes, leaned the flower against my nose and inhaled the sweet, heavy perfume. The petals felt velvety against my skin. "Thank you."

The small card attached read "Sorry for your loss, love Cole."

Tears filled my eyes. No one had given me anything when Omi died. Of course, I had been only six years old. They probably hadn't even thought of me. "You're very sweet." I would have kissed him if it weren't for Wolfie, and the fact that I was sitting in the front and he was in the back.

At the home, we signed in as usual and sanitized our hands. Then, along with Gillian and the new nurse, a short, stocky Mexican-looking dude, Cole and I wheeled and walked almost all the residents into the chapel.

"Make sure none of them wander off during the service," Gillian warned us as we took our own seats at the back.

Two huge arrangements of flowers framed the aisle but no coffin sat at the front. I peered around for any sign of Johann, a portrait photo or maybe an urn sitting near the altar. Nothing. We'd lost the last bit that was left of him and now it was as though there was no trace or reminder that he'd ever lived.

In the front row there was a huge man with a beard and long hair, all silver, like Santa Claus. Next to him sat a chubby lady with ruby-bright hair and lots of rings. The rest of the chapel was filled with the inmates in a variety of sleep stages.

The minister giving the service was from Newfoundland and the only thing that kept my mind in the room while he spoke was his accent, the way he kept saying "byes" for boys and referring to "my son" when he was talking to everyone in general. He called for Johann's son and up stood Santa. "And now Siegfried Schwartz will say a few words about his poppy."

That's when the screen rolled down out of the ceiling and I noticed a computer on a chair next to the chubby lady.

Siegfried used a remote control to flip the slides on a PowerPoint of Johann's life. First he showed photos of Johann in his German uniform while he told us about his secret work helping Jewish families escape from Germany. He met and fell in love with Lydia, one of the girls he had assisted at a reunion of the seventeen families in New York City after the war. Siegfried showed a photo of the groom and happy bride.

Lydia looked a bit like a tiny version of Alexis with her great golden hair and pale blue eyes. When she and Johann found they couldn't have children, they adopted Siegfried, Rolf, and Helga.

He flipped to pictures of Johann's children when they were young and then when they were adults with their families. Unfortunately, they had all moved to Australia and couldn't visit. A whole dynasty on another continent. The last slide was a photo of a different Johann, an older man looking at something in the distance. I dabbed at the corner of my eyes. I wished I could have known him then or that he could have remained that person with the sharp gaze.

Siegfried told one last story about how he once walked through a park late at night with his dad and they came upon a bunch of teenagers near a bonfire who were being questioned by a couple of police officers. The teens were mouthing off and the police shoved one to the ground. "Dad stopped when he saw the constable remove a club from his holster. He stepped closer to the policeman, and even though Dad was smaller than the constable, he placed a hand on his shoulder.

"Good evening, Officer. I hope you don't mind if my son and I watch how our police services work in a democratic country. It will remind me of all the reasons I came to Canada."

Siegfried choked up at this point and with that last image still on the screen, the organ played something from Bach.

I would have joined Siegfried's silent weeping except at that moment Susan started laughing hysterically.

"Shut up!" Jeannette elbowed her hard and Susan screeched.

Gillian rushed to take her away.

"Wow," I said to Cole. "I can't believe how sad I feel that I never met Johann before. What a wonderful person."

"But isn't it great? He's free. A man like that deserves to live out his last years with more dignity." Cole grabbed the handles to his grandmother's wheelchair.

I nodded. I couldn't feel sad about him dying, not in the state he was in.

"See you in a bit?" Cole asked.

"Yup. I'll find you."

Siegfried Schwartz walked over just as I was helping Marlene and Fred to their feet. I picked up Susan's baby doll from the floor, and found I had to screw its head back on.

"Hello." He held out his hand and I had to shift the doll to my other arm in order to shake it. "I understand you were very kind to my father and I just want to thank you for that." He held onto my hand for a moment and I reached up to hug him.

"I'm sorry for your loss . . . not this one. But the disease . . . you know?"

"Yes. I'm glad my father is together with my mother once more. It's a wonderful Christmas gift."

He introduced Linda, the red-haired lady, as his wife and she smiled and shook my hand too.

They both strolled along with me to lockup as I guided another lady in a walker. Along the way, Siegfried thanked everyone for the good care they gave his father.

It was lunchtime now and the chef had cooked a special turkey dinner for the day. I made sure Susan kept eating so she wouldn't call out and annoy Jeannette.

Afterwards Cole and I sat by the courtyard window with his grandmother and Jeannette. Cole gave them each a candy and it seemed to make both of them sleepy because next thing we knew, they had slumped in their chairs. Jeannette to the left, Helen to the right.

"I'm jealous." Cole told me when he saw the Schwartzes leave. "I thought Gillian was calling about Grandma on Thursday."

"How long do the doctors give her?"

"They can't predict. The average Alzheimer's patient lives eight to ten years after they first get symptoms."

"From my project research, I remember even longer — fourteen years."

"I've heard of them living twenty years. Way too long. I remember when Grandma first got diagnosed, she cried and cried."

"I can't imagine how I'd feel if someone told me I had it."

"That's when she made me promise. Once she didn't know anything about what was going on around her — I should help her 'go.'" Cole stared down at his grandmother's hands. One was gnarled tightly into a fist, the nails digging into the skin. He reached over and smoothed his hand over it, trying to loosen the fingers.

"Oh, come on. How exactly are you supposed to do that? Bring in a gun?"

He shook his head. "I think she hoped for some tube I could disconnect. Or some extra pill I could give her. I don't know."

"Well, if there was something that easy, maybe . . ."

"But my mother insisted on extraordinary measures."

"What does that mean exactly?"

"It means if Grandma stops eating, my mother still wants a feeding tube inserted. If she gets pneumonia, she still wants her to receive antibiotics . . . My mother just can't let her go."

"But she doesn't even visit her." I shook my head. "She shouldn't have a say. Your grandmother should make the choices."

Cole was quiet for a bit. Then suddenly, he perked up. "Hey, do you want to come to a movie with me? That new Christmas one. It sounds sappy enough to cheer us up."

"I wish I could. It sounds like what I need." *Just go then,* a little voice told me. "But I promised Donovan I would meet him at the mall. Wolfie's dropping me off."

"Of course." Cole stroked his grandma's hand some more.

Looking back now, I think everything could have gone differently if I had just listened to the little voice inside me.

chapter fourteen

My lawyer stands to question Cole's mother now. "First, I'm sure I represent the entire court when I say we're deeply sorry for your loss."

"Thank you," Mrs. Demers says.

Michael bows his head, waits for a beat and then continues. "Earlier, Mr. Dougal asked you what the prognosis for your mother-in-law's condition was, and I'm a little unclear on that. Would you kindly explain to the court what Alzheimer's disease means in general?"

"Certainly. Plaque builds up around the brain cells and the patient loses reasoning ability."

"Does it progress beyond that? I mean, the brain controls all our functions . . ."

"Objection," the buzzard calls. "The witness is not a medical expert."

"Your Honour, I'm not asking for an expert testimony. I only want to know the witness's understanding of the disease. It could affect her attitude towards the defendant."

"Overruled," the judge answers. "You may proceed, Counsel."

"Mrs. Demers, more specifically, is dementia the only

symptom of Alzheimer's?" Michael's eyebrows are up and his head is tilted.

Mrs. Demers frowns and shifts her gaze around the room. Finally she answers. "No. My mother-in-law not only forgot where her keys were, she also forgot who we were. She had recently forgotten how to walk and stopped talking for the most part."

He cups his hand around his chin. "What about swallowing? Had she forgotten how to swallow?"

"She was having difficulty, but Cole was feeding her so obviously she could still manage."

Michael nods. "Is it true your mother-in-law loved sweets, in particular, candy?"

"Yes. Even when she lived with us she was always sneaking treats into the house, sharing them with Cole. It was always their little joke on us."

More nods, he turns slightly to the jury and back. "And do you know if Helen could suck on a candy?"

Her face turns pink. "She was not supposed to have any. She's diabetic."

Michael McCann smiles patiently. "Let's suppose it's a sugar-free candy, then. Do you know if she could manage one of those or not?"

Claudine stays quiet and turns a deeper shade of pink.

"Mrs. Demers?"

"No, I don't know."

"Isn't it true that the only time you visited your mother-in-law was to see her after Sunny coloured her hair?"

"No!" she shouts. The judge looks at her and she quiets down. "I saw her at Christmas."

"Is Alzheimer's disease considered a fatal disease?"

"Yes. But with good care, a patient can live five to ten years, sometimes even twenty after diagnosis."

Michael flips through his notes. "How long did you say your mother had it?"

"Four years."

"It seems her disease was progressing rapidly."

"Objection. Speculation," the buzzard calls.

"Sustained."

"Was your mother-in-law in the final stage of the disease?" Michael asks in a louder voice.

"I don't know," she snaps.

"Did her doctor ask you to sign for palliative care only?" he asks more gently.

"Yes."

"And what did you decide?"

"I did not sign. They were to use every measure to keep her alive. Life is sacred to us."

"But Cole felt differently." His voice is louder again.

"Yes. No."

"Which is it, Mrs. Demers? Didn't he argue for you to sign for palliative care only? No heroic measures?"

"Yes."

"You said earlier that Sonja broke your son's heart. Isn't it true that you blame Sonja for Cole's accident?"

"The driver was charged with reckless driving. I blame him."

"But your son left Paradise Manor before Sonja arrived. If he had waited and gone out with her, he wouldn't have been riding in that spot when that driver answered his cell. Isn't that right, Mrs. Demers?"

"Yes," she hisses, eyes burning into me.

"Would he have been wearing a helmet if he hadn't had his hair styled for his night out?"

"Definitely. He always wore his helmet."

I shake my head, remembering what I saw about the accident on television on Valentine's night: the bike with the crumpled frame, the car with the smashed headlight and broken fender. "An accident that could have been avoided," the reporter had said as he stood in front of the car, "if the driver had not been speaking on his cell phone and the bike rider had just worn his helmet." Of course Cole's mom blamed me.

"Earlier you made a judgment about the character of my client. I wonder, had you even met Sonja Ehret before today?"

Mrs. Demers shakes her head. "No."

"No further questions."

She made a judgment that affected my whole life. Did the jury understand? All I ever wanted was to satisfy my volunteer requirement.

The Fourteenth Visit — twelve hours left

Turns out Paradise Manor is not just for seniors. A man my dad's age checked into the room that used to belong to Johann Schwartz. I think he was a biker because his first visitor rode up on a Harley Davidson. He brought a box of doughnuts and Jeannette said she never got any. So guess who walked over to the coffee shop and bought another box, Mr. Brooks?

As I walked to the front entrance of Paradise Manor on that Monday, a black and chrome motorcycle roared up, the cold air making the exhaust freeze in a huge cloud around it. Geez, did they make those things with snow tires? I couldn't help staring as the rider parked it. He took off his helmet and what little hair he had flattened around a bald spot and hung down his back in a ponytail. He was a big guy, the size of a fridge, and he wore a leather jacket and chaps over faded jeans. Bending down, he removed a coffee-shop bag from the hard, black box attached to the side of his seat and followed in behind me.

I signed the visitor book at reception as usual, but he swaggered in ahead. Nobody stopped him. As dirty as he could have been from riding, no one nagged him to sanitize his hands either. Was it because they didn't bother adults, or were they afraid of bikers? As I looked back to check Katherine's reaction I saw that she was just returning to her seat at that moment.

The biker keyed in the code and then held the door open for me. He strode ahead when I stopped to chat with Jeannette. She sat in a chair along the corridor near the dining room, her shoulders hunched. "Hi, how are you?" I asked her, dumping my coat on the chair next to her.

She barely glanced up; her lips moved but I didn't hear what she said. It was easy to see she was feeling miserable.

That's when I noticed the cast on her foot. "Hey, what happened there?"

She looked at me, sneering. "You kicked me."

I thought about that one for a second. Did she really think I had hurt her or was she teasing? Would she snap if I denied it?

I didn't want to take a chance. "Well, I'm sorry about that." I quickly moved on. A lot of the old folk already hovered near the dining room, but I went to see if I could help the staff bring the rest out. I saw that new Mexican nurse, Ambrose they called him, pushing Mrs. Demers. Where was Cole today?

I went into Marlene's room and helped her down the hall till Fred joined us. Then I coaxed Susan to dinner by asking her if her baby was hungry.

I didn't even look in Johann Schwartz's room; I couldn't bear to see it empty. But then I saw the biker dude pushing a wheelchair out. The guy sitting in it looked in better shape than the biker. He had lots of dark hair, and appeared slim — though it's hard to tell in a wheelchair sometimes. He wore a long-sleeved shirt tucked into some wrinkle-free Dockers. The biker's arms were bare to the shoulder now that he'd removed his jacket. On his left arm he had a tattoo of some kind of wizard, on his right a castle tower.

He wheeled his buddy into the dining room and sat with him as he ate.

Meanwhile, Cole had finally arrived. "Hi, Sunny!" He smiled at me and then bent over to kiss his grandmother. "Sorry I'm late Grandma. Mom made me take the bus because of the ice today."

"Sunny, can you see if you can get Jeannette in?" Gillian asked me as she sat down with Marlene and Fred.

"I don't know. She was mad at me before," I told her.

"Please try. You know you're her favourite. Pretend you just arrived. She won't remember that she was mad."

I stood up and headed out to the hall. To my surprise she wasn't at her spot by the window. I kept walking. She wasn't in the common room or along the corridor anywhere. I checked her room. Not there.

Had she escaped? She seemed bright enough to figure out the exit code by watching visitors punch it in. I turned back to report her missing. But just then she rolled out of Johann

Schwartz's room holding what looked like a box of doughnuts.

"Jeannette. Don't eat any of those. It's time for dinner," I told her.

"There's none left. He gave everyone a doughnut except me. There were honey crullers and sour cream glazed. Even a chocolate double dip."

Interesting that she could remember them in such detail. I shook my head. "You don't want any of those anyway. They're so bad for your figure."

Jeannette's head drooped and she started to cry.

I wasn't sure how to handle this, so I tried to distract her. "Hey, Jeannette, you never said anything about my new dress." It was the earth-toned gypsy skirt that went so well with my coffee-bean necklace. She had loved it the last time I wore it. I did a little twirl in front of her. "What do you think?"

"We never get doughnuts here."

"What are you talking about? You get stuff that's way better. Remember all the squares and cookies at the party?"

"I like doughnuts."

"Maybe you'll have a nice dessert with supper today. C'mon, let's check together." I pushed her wheelchair towards the dining room, stopped just outside the door, and read from the bulletin board menu. "Lime Jell-O or orange sherbet. Doesn't that sound good?"

"No. I want a honey cruller." She suddenly jabbed her good heel against the floor and the wheelchair stopped.

"Can you warn me when you're going to do that? Otherwise you could break your other foot."

"I'm not going in there."

"Listen, I'll walk to the store and pick up a dozen. But you have to go eat dinner first."

"You promise me?" Her tiny, dark eyes focused on me like a hamster's on a sunflower seed.

"Fine, sure. I just have to tell Gillian where I'm going." I pushed Jeannette to her normal spot. Gillian wasn't in the room anymore, so I told Cole and took an order for his favourite doughnut as well.

Off I went, grabbing my coat from the chair as I left. The coffee shop was about four long blocks away and the roads were icy. I couldn't believe Cole needed to be told not to ride his bike today. Couldn't believe that biker either. It took me a while to baby-step my way over there.

The doorbell tinkled as I walked into the coffee shop. There's nothing quite as good as the smell of coffee and doughnuts. Sweet and light, rich and mellow. Both smell way better than they taste. I don't even like eating the doughnuts, never mind drinking the pencil-shaving coffee, but choosing the doughnuts relaxes me. It's like arranging a flower bouquet or decorating for a party.

As I stood by the counter gazing at the rows of doughnuts through the glass, I suddenly remembered doing this with Omi. She liked the apple fritters. She gave me bites of hers and asked if they weren't the most delicious thing. Just looking at them made me feel loved again.

When the line shifted so that it was my turn, I ordered four apple fritters (in case the other old people liked them too), four crullers, two sour cream glazed, and two of the new cherry chocolate flower-shaped ones Cole said he liked.

Back I went, slipping and sliding all the way. By the time I returned to the dining room, most of the residents were finishing their sherbet. Jeannette had fallen asleep in her chair. I didn't see the biker or his friend anywhere.

"I'd like a doughnut," Marlene said.

"Heck, so would I," Fred agreed.

I passed a few around. Cole snuck an apple fritter for his grandmother. Then I placed the rest of the box in Jeannette's lap. Maybe she'd forget or maybe she wouldn't, but a promise is a promise, and I wanted her to wake up to the little party I had arranged for her on her lap. I wheeled her to a spot by the courtyard window and Cole wheeled his grandma alongside of us. She was asleep, too, by now.

"Hey, that reminds me. Have you seen *Insurrection II*?" Cole asked.

"Don't tell me there's another one out." With the two old folks dozing, it was nice to just talk at a normal voice level with each other. "I don't like action flicks."

"You like comedy and romance? *Just Not Into Prom*'s going to be at the Silver Screen next Friday." He looked at me hopefully.

I could see where this was going. He was working up the courage to ask me out. Too bad he was so easy to dodge at this point. "The mom dies of cancer in that. How's that a comedy?"

"I dunno. The trailer showed some funny bits."

"Cole, my mother's in remission."

"Oh my God, Sunny! I'm sorry." He slammed his forehead with his hand.

"It's okay. You didn't know. And she's doing pretty good now."

"Forget the movie idea." He turned to face me then and I could tell something serious was coming. "February 18 we have a Valentine's dance at our school."

"Is it a formal?" I asked.

"Semi," he answered. "You saw me at Halloween. You

know I'm a great dancer."

I giggle. I knew I could have a lot of fun with him. "Look, Cole, you know I'm still going out with Donovan."

"I don't mind. I mean if we just go as friends. You don't have to tell Donovan."

Just as friends, which we definitely are, I thought. That would work for me. Would Donny agree? I mean he wouldn't see Cole as a threat, scrawny and messy haired as he was. Donovan would recognize instantly that Cole wasn't my type. My usual type, anyway. "Can I just think about it? If I broke off with Donovan, I'd go out with you for sure. But I'm not a cheat, you know?"

"Of course not." Cole smiled. "Well, doesn't look like these two are waking up. I'll just put Grandma in her room and go."

"See you at the door." I wheeled Jeannette back to her room, hoping she still craved doughnuts when she woke up.

Then I waved goodbye to Cole and headed home where — surprise! — my parents were already serving up dinner. Nothing much was happening at the condo office since they'd had their annual meeting the Friday before, so they'd left work early.

Mom served *rouladen* and red cabbage with a cucumber salad for supper, all my favourite foods.

"This is delicious," I told her. "And you made it so fast!"

"With the help of the delicatessen," she said. "Not the salad, but all the rest. I just heated it up, Sunny. But thank you." She smiled at me. My mom's smile spread light over the world.

It had been a great day. I felt good about how I handled Jeannette. Maybe forced volunteer work was okay after all. It opened your eyes to helping different kinds of people, ones you wouldn't normally meet.

Then the phone rang. I checked call display to see if it was Donny. *Paradise Manor*, the window read. I picked up.

"Sonja?"

"Mrs. Johnson."

"Yes, hello Sonja. Did you give Mrs. Demers a box of doughnuts this evening?" You could tell by her tone that this wasn't a happy call.

"No, of course not."

"Well, there was an empty box in her room and Sheila said you brought them in."

"Yes, I bought some for Jeannette, but I never gave any to Helen."

"Well, Helen must have eaten a quite a few because she went into a diabetic coma."

"What?" I squawked and then took a breath. "Is she okay?"

"We're hoping she'll pull out of it. You know how frail they all are." Her tone sounded like she was blaming that on me, too.

"Mrs. Johnson, did Sheila not see that Hell's Angel guy visiting the new resident? He brought doughnuts in too. And Jeannette was crying 'cause he never gave her any."

"Are you sure you didn't leave *your* box around for Mrs. Demers to eat?"

"No. Like I said, I'm sure it was the biker 'cause I took the rest home. My brother loves doughnuts." It was a quick half lie. Wolfie does enjoy his sweets.

"No one mentioned a biker to me. I'll check the guest book. Maybe I can call him."

"Oh, he didn't sign. I walked in right behind him so I know." Funny how the truth sounds like a lie sometimes. I can lie way better than I tell the truth.

"And he rode a motorcycle in this weather," she said.

"Yeah, even Cole knew better than to bike in, so it just goes to show you."

"What, Sonja?"

"What do you mean, what?" I asked.

"You said it showed me something. What?"

"That the biker had no sense. He didn't think not to leave the doughnuts where Helen couldn't reach them. He wouldn't have known about her diabetes anyway."

"All right. I'll ask the staff about him. No more sweets for the patients, Sunny."

I crossed my fingers. "Sure." I swallowed. "I hope Mrs. Demers gets better and gets out of that wheelchair, too."

"That's not likely, and you and Cole know that. Good night." She hung up.

I rolled my eyes. "Good night," I answered into the dead phone.

The moment I got off the phone with Mrs. Johnson, I called Cole. "I'm so sorry about your grandma. You know I never meant for her to get into those doughnuts. I just wanted Jeannette to have them when she woke up in case she remembered me promising them."

"Don't worry about it," Cole spit the words out like he was angry. "If she dies, you'll have done her a big favour."

"What do you mean?"

Cole lowered his voice as though he was afraid someone might be listening. "Well, you know she asked me to help her, uh, 'go' when the time came that she couldn't do anything for herself. She can't even talk, Sunny. Sometimes she doesn't even know I'm with her. Only . . ."

He stayed quiet for so long that I wondered if the phone had died. "Cole? Cole, are you there?"

"Yeah, I'm here. I just had to wait till my mother left the room." His voice broke. "Sunny, she asked me to kill her and I can't do it. No matter how bad it gets, I just can't."

"Aw, Cole." Over the phone you just can't give hugs. I sighed. "She shouldn't have asked you. It wasn't fair."

"But she's done so much for me. She helped me with homework, made my lunches, took me on fieldtrips, paid for my exchange trip to France, set aside money for my education . . . she only asked this one thing."

"Which is huge. Too huge. How could anyone ask that of you?"

"Because we both knew how bad it would get. She would have done something herself earlier if I hadn't promised."

"So what, you feel you lied to her?"

"Yes, and that I've let her down."

"I don't know. People make such a big deal about honesty. I think you just can't always tell the truth." I racked my brains for something better to say, something to comfort him. "Any moment researchers may come up with a cure. Then you'll be the big hero for not keeping a promise."

"She's too far gone for any miracle."

"Maybe. But how would you have even done it? There aren't any tubes or plugs to pull."

"I dunno. Sleeping pills. Maybe a box of doughnuts."

"Don't even kid."

"Doesn't matter how. I'm too big a coward. Every visit I give her a candy and half hope she will choke on it. The other half still hopes she'll somehow get better again."

He became quiet again and so did I. Finally I had to say something. "Listen, I told Mrs. Johnson that it was the biker's doughnuts your grandmother ate."

"Oh. What if she calls him?"

"Well, it could have been his box your grandma got into. How the heck did she get anybody's doughnuts, is what I want to know. He didn't sign in so Mrs. Johnson doesn't know his name. If he visits again soon, I could be in trouble. But I've served eighteen hours towards my volunteer credit. I only have twelve left."

"Twelve hours."

"Don't sound like that. We'll still be friends after that."

"Friends."

"Are you going to keep repeating everything I say?"

"No."

"Good. Anyway, I told Mrs. Johnson I took the box of doughnuts away with me. If she asks, can you please just go along with that story?"

"I already did. I mean I told her a biker brought some. I said I never saw you with any."

"Thanks, Cole." I sighed again. "I'm sorry about your grandma. I mean, not just about the doughnuts . . . the Alzheimer's. Her asking that of you. It isn't fair."

"No. Nothing is. Bye, Sunny."

I hesitated an extra moment. I wanted to tell him I would definitely break up with Donovan very soon. There was still hope for him. But I just wasn't sure yet. I didn't know if I could face school without Donovan on my arm. He made me feel like I fit in. And about some things I really can't lie. "Bye, Cole."

chapter fifteen

The next person the buzzard calls up is the Mexican nurse. Turns out his whole name is Ambrosio Flores. Funny how I never paid much attention to him before and now he gets a big say in how my life goes from here on in. He's dressed respectfully, with a pinstriped white shirt and a burgundy tie paired with navy slacks. Take note jury, you can dress well on a budget. He's got a head of that great blue-black hair that unfortunately greys so quickly, and skin that looks one shade darker than a tan. His eyes are a soulful chocolate colour. He swears in on the Bible.

"Mr. Flores, how long have you been working for Paradise Manor?"

"I have been working for the Manor for one-and-a-half years." Ambrose speaks a bit formally with just the tiniest hint of an accent when he stretches out his Es.

"In your job you were able to observe Miss Ehret in her volunteer role. How did she treat the seniors?"

"Oh, she was very kind to them. She talked quite a bit with Miss Jeannette and I remember she fixed Miss Susan's doll many times."

"How did Cole act towards his grandmother, when you

saw them all together?"

"When I came, Mrs. Demers was already pretty far gone into the dementia. She did not talk or even feed herself. Cole was the only person who visited her on my shift. He did slip her a lot of sweets, which we were instructed not to give her on account of the diabetes."

"And what about Sonja? Did she give Mrs. Demers things she wasn't supposed to have?

"Yes. She would get extra cookies to give Cole so he could slip them to Grandmama. And she brought in a box of doughnuts."

"Can you describe any problems these extra treats may have caused?"

"After the doughnuts, Mrs. Demers went into a diabetic coma."

"No further questions."

Sometimes I wish Cole's grandma had died in that coma. Between me and the biker, surely Mrs. Johnson would have had *him* charged for the death. But of course, she didn't die. It's always the person you least expect who goes first.

The Fifteenth Visit — ten hours left

I helped with another funeral, Mr. Brooks. I can't believe Susan died. Besides carrying the baby doll around all the time and ranting about strange things, she seemed pretty healthy. Yeah, and I brought my boyfriend. In case Mrs. J. complains, I thought they liked having a bigger crowd for these send-offs.

The next day Donny wanted to go to the mall, but I didn't. "I've got homework."

"I'll help." He drew in close and stroked my neck. "Come to my house. I've got Kinect ballroom dancing." His dad worked for a game company so Donovan always had the absolute latest.

"Can I bring Alexis?"

"Aw, why?" He dropped his hand from me. "We never spend any time alone anymore."

"Because I wanna tell my mom I hung out with Alexis after school and be sort of telling the truth."

"If you loved me you'd just tell your mother where to go."

I rolled my eyes at him. "Oh, like I don't all the time. Look, there's Alexis." I waved. "Alexis, Alexis." I ran to catch up to her. "Come to Donovan's with me."

"What, to watch you guys make out?"

"No!" I gave her shoulder a shove. Then I whispered into her ear. "So I don't have to be alone with him."

"Then break up with him."

"Lexie, please?" I only used her baby name for special occasions.

"Fine." She turned on her heel and waved at Donny like he was her best friend.

"You coming?" Donny asked and when she nodded, he acted pleased. "All right then, let's go." He gave her his most charming smile, dimples and all.

You see, people deceive in all kinds of ways, not just breaking promises or telling outright lies. And it worked out to be a great afternoon because of it.

We drove home together. If I broke up with Donovan I'd miss having a boyfriend with a car. Alexis and I worked on our poetry assignments while Donny made us crêpes with mozzarella cheese and raspberry jam, my favourite. If I broke up with Donny, I'd miss having someone cook for me. I wondered if Cole knew how to make crêpes.

Later we waltzed, and did the cha-cha and the rumba against the competing couple on the wall screen. Donny made me feel like I could float to the music. Even Alexis had a good time when we switched places. Cole's dancing at the Manor's Halloween party had looked choppy and awkward.

It was January. I still had a month to break up with Donovan if I wanted to go to the Valentine's dance with Cole. But maybe I didn't really want to break up.

"Donny, what would you say if I helped a friend by going to a dance with him?" I asked while we were doing an easy two-step.

Donovan missed a beat. "What do you mean, 'help'? Who is this guy?"

From over his shoulder, I could see Alexis making silent scream faces at me.

"Oh just that geeky kid I volunteer with at the home. Haven't I told you about Cole before?"

"No. I'd remember if you had. I'd have to meet him." Donny twirled me then and we beat the couple on the screen. "You know, Sunny, you may think a guy wants to be your friend. But honestly, if he's human, how could he not want to be more?"

Alexis took her turn dancing with Donovan then. "Don't worry, Cole is nothing compared to you," she told him. "But you should go to Paradise Manor anyway. You can see how good Sunny is with the old people."

Okay, now she was being too helpful.

"Yeah, Sunny, I should probably come one time," he said as he swung Alexis around.

I rolled my eyes. "Bringing a boyfriend to a volunteer job, my teacher's gonna love that."

But there was no talking Donovan out of coming to the home once Alexis put it in his head. He joked about wanting to meet my other boyfriend and seeing how all the track pants he lifted fit on the old guys. I didn't know what to do until Gillian Halliday called about Susan's death. "Don't be sad for her, Sunny. Her heart stopped beating in the middle of the night. She went to bed and never woke up."

"I just didn't think she'd be the next to go." My voice did a little hiccup and I stopped for a second. I couldn't help it. You can't just not be sad when someone tells you not to be. "Johann, I could have predicted. Mrs. Demers seems the oldest and sickest . . . and she wants to die."

"It doesn't always work out like that. We never know whose time is next."

Blah, blah, live every day like it's your last . . . I changed the subject to stop her blather. "Can I bring someone?"

"Alexis? Sure," Gillian answered.

"No, Donovan. He's my boyfriend. He just wants to see what I do there."

"But I thought you and Cole . . . Never mind, that's fine, Sunny. Bring him along."

So I called Donovan next and he seemed bizarrely excited to be accompanying me to a funeral. I wanted to call Cole to warn him, but I just couldn't work up the nerve.

Donny dressed up beautifully for the occasion — he always knew how to do that — dark overcoat covering a dark suit saved from being too funereal by a rose-coloured shirt and silver-and-mauve striped tie. We arrived early.

A Nubreeze smell hung in the air and the reception area

was decked out in yellow and white mums. Obviously they had spiffed up the place for the event. I directed him to sanitize and sign in, then I punched in the lockup code and we entered the Alzheimer's ward.

"Are you a movie star? You're certainly a handsome young man." A woman I didn't recognize grabbed Donny's arm. "Come and see my cat."

He grinned at her and winked back at me. "Sure, I'd love to see it."

Standing behind her, I shook my head and mouthed, "No pets allowed." Still I followed them to her room and stood in the doorway. That lady owned a battery-powered breathing cat with real fur. What kind of fur was that? It was so creepy. I let him continue ahead, and visit with Marlene and Jeannette, too. He would take their arms like a groomsman takes a bridesmaid's. I was proud of him. He was so gallant.

Meanwhile, I helped Ambrose push the wheelchair folk into the chapel. I'd been lulled into thinking this would be another PowerPoint-type celebration of life. But it all felt different. An artificial sweetness hung over the air. Two huge flowerpots stood at the front overflowing with pink lilies.

Behind those lilies lay a coffin, no lid on top.

I gulped at the air but couldn't breathe.

A huge arrangement of red roses draped over the bottom half. The top part was open to Susan, lying eyes closed and lip slightly curved upward.

I still couldn't get any air in and the top part of my head seemed to be floating away.

Suddenly, Cole was there catching me as my knees buckled. Ambrose quickly pushed a chair underneath me. "If you're feeling faint, Miss, put your head between your knees."

"I'm okay. I'm okay."

"Take deep breaths." Cole squatted in front of me holding both of my arms. Gradually, the room stopped moving and the floating sensation stopped. "Do you want me to take you to see her?" Cole asked gently. "Maybe it will help."

I shook my head, inhaled deeply, and felt relieved when I could let the breath out again and continue.

"It's a way of saying goodbye. Closure, you know. Just try with me." He held onto my hand.

Finally I nodded. Gripping his arm tightly, I stood up and walked to the coffin. I concentrated on my breathing. Susan wasn't wearing her glasses. Her eyes were closed as though she were sleeping, so that didn't seem too weird. Something did feel unnatural, though. It was that near smile on her face.

It made it seem like this was all some big joke and she was just pretending behind those closed eyes.

"Wake up," I whispered to her. "Your baby's crying."

"There, there." Cole squeezed my arm. "She's lucky she went before she got worse."

"Oh yeah, she's crazy lucky. Too bad she didn't buy a ticket to the lottery before she died." I choked on a sob then and Cole wrapped me in his arms.

"It's okay. It's okay, Sunny." He patted my shoulder. "She's at peace now. You've got to see that."

I sniffed and disentangled myself. I stared. "Maybe. She does look relaxed. Less wrinkled. Like she's had a facelift, even." A half laugh, half sob bubbled up.

"Let's go back and help the others in," Cole suggested and we walked out to the lockup again.

Calmer, I headed down one hall and he went on through the other. I pushed Jeannette's wheelchair to the chapel and met him pushing his grandmother's.

Donny, for his part, escorted the cat lady down the aisle. She seemed to be flirting with him.

"Don't make a big deal. Let her have her fantasy with him," Cole told me. "That one second she's enjoying is her whole life right now."

But Donny set her in a chair and returned to us.

"So you're the guy who's trying to steal my girl," Donny said when we all met up in the back row.

"Behave." I punched his shoulder. "Donovan, this is Cole; Cole, this is Donovan." I turned and saw Cole as if with Donny's eyes.

Cole looked awkward, as usual, wearing the same suit as last funeral. He must have biked in because he had a serious case of helmet hair. He blushed as Donovan pumped at his hand. Was Donny crushing it?

I stared at him, throwing stop-it signals his way. Finally Donny released Cole's hand.

"Pleased to meet you," Cole said. We sat down to wait for the service.

There were no more people than last time, but hymns were sung — or maybe howled would be a better way to describe it. Donny and Cole sang along, Donny in baritone, Cole in squeaking adolescent. I couldn't open my mouth. I never sang in front of Donny, ever.

No one spoke on Susan's behalf, although our Newfoundland minister read a bit about her from his notes. The service ended quickly.

Afterwards we stayed to help feed the old people back in the dining room. Donny stayed patient and charming the whole time. He offered Cole a lift when we were finished. "I can throw your bike in the trunk, no worries."

Cole turned him down.

Before we left the dining room, I saw Cole unwrap a candy and give it to Mrs. Demers. He kissed her and walked out the door with us.

We all stopped for a moment at the exit to say goodbye.

Donovan started in again. "Listen, Cole, just so we understand each other. You're a real nice guy and all . . . but she's not coming to any dance with you. I don't care if it's as a friend or as a team mascot, for that matter. Do you get me?"

I could see his jaw line was firm. He wasn't joking.

"Yup."

Donny broke into a grin again and clapped his hand on Cole's shoulder. "You sure about that ride? Biking's dangerous in this weather, man."

"Sure, sure."

The one time no one listens to Donny, he's really telling the truth, predicting the future really.

chapter sixteen

"Mr. Flores." The buzzard coughs. "Can you tell the court how Sonja reacted to Susan White's funeral?"

"At first I thought she would faint. The coffin was open, you know, and she told her friend she had never seen a dead body before. I told her to put her head down between her knees."

Bored, the prosecutor looks off to the judge. "This friend was Cole Demers?"

Yes, Cole. He was a good volunteer, too. She was also with another boy, taller — I never saw him before. But he stayed at the back and Cole took Miss Sunny up to see the body of Miss Susan."

"Did you happen to hear what she said?"

"Yes. She said Miss Susan looked nice, nicer in the coffin than she did alive."

Someone groans in the jury.

"Order!" the judge warns.

Oh man, this is so unfair. It sounds like I thought everyone was better off dead. It wasn't true. I was all nerves that day and nothing that came out of my mouth made sense. I was giving the mortician a compliment. I told Alexis later that every old person should go to the funeral home for makeovers. I mean they totally got rid of Susan's wrinkles and she was smiling so peacefully.

I feel tired of it all and want to lay my head down on the oak rail in front of me. The four beige walls seem to squeeze the air out of the courtroom. One of the bearded guys in the back row yawns and I feel an urge tugging at my jaw too.

My lawyer Michael McCann stands up now. The yawning stops and I can't help noticing that the jogging-suit lady kind of leans forward for him. Will we get a not-guilty verdict from her just because he's cute? Whatever. I need it.

"Mr. Flores, you mentioned earlier that Mrs. Demers was pretty far gone when you began working in the lockup unit. How did you like working with her?" He grips the wooden railing in front of him.

"Oh, she was a sweetheart. She always thanked me whenever I did anything."

"She thanked you . . . but I thought she couldn't talk."

"Most of the time she didn't. But I guess thanking was a habit that stayed behind. The patients have good moments sometimes."

"Can you describe any other good moments?"

"Oh, yes. Mrs. Demers had been silent for a while but we still talked all the time around the patients whether they answered or not. She seemed blue one day, so I told her how I was missing my family in Florida but it was such a long drive from here. I didn't know if my car could make it. And suddenly she said, as clear as a bell, 'Take a plane.'"

"Really? But that meant she must have understood you, too. What about physically? She used a wheelchair. Was she mobile on her own?"

"No. She stopped walking just when I started working in that unit."

"This is a characteristic of Alzheimer's though, correct?"

"Yes. She didn't have a stroke, or severe enough arthritis to cause it. But then when I was getting her up for breakfast one morning, she just walked into the bathroom and brushed her own teeth. One time only, and then not again."

"She never stood up on her own legs and walked again for you. Is it possible she may have walked on her own when you weren't there?"

"Nobody told me about it, but it's possible."

"She could have done it when nobody was watching, perhaps to visit another resident's room or to help herself to some sweets?"

The doughnuts that the biker brought in . . . or the ones in Jeannette's room. The candies that she choked on.

Ambrose's eyes shift to look into mine for just a moment. I feel myself starting to smile and stop.

"It is possible. But it is not so likely. Someone would have seen her."

Everyone was too busy, you liar. My doughnuts were resting on Jeannette's lap, they didn't fly into Helen Demers's mouth on their own.

"When you started working on the first floor last year did you ever notice a biker visiting the resident Frank Conner?"

"Oh, yes. I talked to him about his chopper. It was a beautiful machine."

"And did he visit other residents' rooms offering them doughnuts or just visiting?

"I'm not sure, but I did see him carry in a box."

Okay, so those doughnuts are still a big strike against

me, despite my lawyer's questions. All I tried to do was keep Jeannette happy. Had I just waited, Jeannette would have forgotten about the treats too. The hands on the clock move slowly into position, the short one nudges the four first, the long one finally hits the twelve. Four o'clock. It's no surprise when the judge calls it a day. "Court is adjourned. We will meet again tomorrow at ten o'clock." Up, slowly, like a big black bird fluffing his feathers. The court clerk tells everyone to rise and we wait while the judge and jury leave. Then I follow with my parents.

As usual, we head back to the condo office. Wolfgang's on the phone when we arrive. Mom tackles a stack of mail in her in-box and Dad just sits down and sighs.

"What's going to happen to me?" I ask him.

"What do you mean? They will find you innocent and you will move on with your life."

"Do you think?"

Schwizt! Mom slits open an envelope, fast and sure, stacking it in a new pile. *Schwizt!*

Dad shrugs his shoulders.

Mom stops and points her opener at me. "All this time we have been listening to the witnesses for the prosecution." She shakes the opener. "When we hear from the witnesses on your side, things will be different. You'll see."

"Mom, I just can't tell if the jury likes me. Some people think everything I do is evil, no matter what I say. Look at Mrs. Johnson."

"Some people are very stupid." *Schwizt, schwizt!* Even faster.

"What do you think? Are the jury members smart?" I look first at my mother and she returns my stare over her glasses.

Schwizt, schwizt!

"You be careful with that," my father warns my mother.

No answer from her. She sees what I see and it's not good. I move my eyes to my father's face.

"Sunny, Sunny. This is not *American Idol*. They will listen and they will need to weigh." He moves his hands up and down like scales. "They must decide things for certain. No doubts." He wags a finger now. "Think how hard it must be to be so sure that you caused this old lady's death."

Schwizt, schwizt. Mom throws the letter opener down. "Impossible! If they do, we will appeal." She jumps up and heads out of the room.

If she's so certain, why does she leave the room? Is she crying? My heart sinks. She had her ultrasound before court this morning. What had it shown? It couldn't have been good news, or we would be celebrating.

"Dad, what happened at the ultrasound today?"

"Nothing. Your mother was at the clinic and the technician refused to say anything. She told Mama to discuss it with her doctor." Dad frowns.

"But they like telling you if it's nothing, don't they?"

He shakes his head. "They are not supposed to tell you *any* results. She has an appointment with the doctor Thursday morning."

But Mom knew she was all clear instantly the last time she had an ultrasound. If Mom has to see her doctor to explain the results, it must mean the cancer is back.

I feel myself floating away from the desk so I grip the edges. Then I take a drink of water. If I am found guilty, I will be gone for two or three years. They could be the last years of Mom's life. Tomorrow will be the toughest witness, too — Mrs.

Johnson. Maybe there is still time to get out of all this.

"Dad, can you call Mr. McCann? I want to change my plea. At least I'll get the lesser sentence."

The Sixteenth Visit — eight hours left

Mrs. Johnson knows my phone number because she called me to complain about the doughnuts that some other guy left behind. I think she could have called to tell me about the quarantine at the residence. A few of the seniors had a flu, so the whole floor was closed off to visitors. The receptionist wouldn't even let me sign in to prove I had been there. It kills a couple of hours of my time riding the bus to and from Paradise Manor. I think this visit should count.

The truth is that when the receptionist stopped me, I was pretty happy. If Cole had asked me right then and there to skip out and go to a movie, I would have taken it all as a sign and said yes.

But instead, Cole told me he had a great immune system, and he wasn't afraid of being around a little flu. He was going to visit his grandma, especially if she was sick.

I have a great immune system, too, and would have liked to cheer the residents up — there's nothing quite as depressing as being alone when you're feeling lousy — but I wasn't sure about my mom's. All those treatments had left her susceptible. What if some strange microbe hitched a ride on me and made her sick?

The phone rang and Katherine Filmore got into a deep discussion. When she needed to check the files at the back to answer a question, Cole made his break for it.

He keyed in the code. "You coming?" He tilted his head towards the door.

I shook my head. I just couldn't risk it.

Then I called Donny and we headed to the mall instead. Instead of browsing stores, I made him apply for some jobs in the food court. I was pretty happy to put him on the road to reform. If he had a job, I was sure he wouldn't be stealing again.

chapter seventeen

Dad makes the call to our lawyer but when he rings back the news is bad. It's too late to bargain. The Crown will not give us a deal anymore. If I change my plea now, the buzzard wants to put me in a young offender's institute for a full two years, with an additional year of probation. There's no other option but to go on.

I can't breathe. I can't sleep that night. The buzzard must be very sure of his case to want to hold out till the end of the trial.

**The Seventeenth Visit — I caught up, Mr. Brooks,
for real, only six hours left**
I stayed a couple of extra hours to play bingo with the seniors today. A resident named Jeannette Ferrier hurt her foot and the pain put her in kind of a slump. Wow, was she serious about her game, though. I did a really good job of cheering her up.

Cole and I rode on the same bus to Paradise Manor on the next Monday. There was a cold weather warning that day and it was already dreary dark. "You didn't take your bike today. Good call," I said when I climbed in and saw him sitting near the front.

"Hey, Sunny. You're using public transit. Excellent. Does that mean you dumped the Neanderthal?"

"No." I smiled as I sat down beside Cole. His hair looked nice today and the dark brown pea coat he wore worked well with his eyes. "You may not like Donovan, but the old ladies sure did."

"Yeah, he flirted and even went to their rooms with them. I think that should mean you can go to the dance with me."

"We'll see." I smiled. He wasn't afraid of Donovan. I was glad.

The bus lumbered and swished through the snow. Cole rubbed at the frosted window with a mitted fist in order to get a view of where we were. "Did you notice *Kidnapping in Athens* is playing at the theatres now? Your boyfriend didn't say we couldn't see a movie together."

I rolled my eyes at Cole. "Honestly, he really doesn't have to itemize."

"When your forty hours are up, do you think you'll still come to Paradise Manor?" His golden eyes held mine for a moment.

"I don't know. I'll miss some of the residents. But Mrs. Johnson really has it in for me."

"She wouldn't if you didn't come just because you have to for school. I mean, if you really volunteer on your own, I'm sure her attitude will change." He peered through the cleared part of the window. "Our stop now." We both stood and Cole pulled the signal rope so the bus driver would know to let us off.

As we walked from the curb to the entrance, he gripped

my elbow so I wouldn't fall. My laced knee-high boots had heels so I needed the help. At least that's what I would tell Donovan if it ever come up somehow. We did the whole signing-in ritual, sterilizing our hands and entering the door-opening code to lockup.

Once inside, we only went a little ways through the hall, till I stopped where Jeannette sat. She didn't look up or say hello.

"I'll see you in the dining room," Cole said as he headed off towards his grandmother's room.

I nodded. "Hey, Jeannette," I said loudly. "I brought you something."

She tilted her head. "What is it? Chocolate?"

"No, better than that." I took out a new lipstick I'd bought — two for one at The Bay. I'd thought of Jeannette immediately. I picked up Plum for me and Strawberry Wine for her. "See?" I unwrapped and uncapped the tube. "Smile for me and I'll put some on you."

She leaned her head back as I rolled the lipstick on. Her pupils were needle-point small and she seemed vague. Was she fading away like Helen Demers?

"There, now you're beautiful for supper. Come, let's go." I pushed her walker towards her.

She stared at it.

"Suppertime, Jeannette. Come on." I patted my hand on one of the handlebars.

Gillian walked by. "Hurry, ladies. We're having bingo at six p.m."

"I don't care about bingo," Jeannette grumbled, but she slowly hoisted herself up on the walker.

"Do you think you can help Jeannette get to her game

and play?" Gillian asked me.

Jeannette turned her head slowly towards me. Her strawberry-wine lips stretched with just the suggestion of a smile. She looked poised to grin if I answered correctly.

"Sure. I love bingo," I lied. "And I'm very lucky." I winked at Jeannette and she tried to straighten. Her eyebrows lifted. If I could do anything to snap her out of her slump and prevent her from sliding down into nothingness, I would do it.

Shepherd's pie or roast chicken for supper. I sat down with Jeannette and coaxed her to eat. She at least got food in its original format. Then I jumped up and visited with Fred and Marlene. Cole gave me a wave with a spoon from where he sat feeding his grandmother. Helen Demers just got plops of colour to eat now.

"Oh, hi Diane," Marlene said. "We're out of bread. Do you think you could pick some up on your way home tonight?"

"Yes. Rye or whole wheat?"

Cole rolled his eyes and shook his head.

Marlene's brow furrowed.

"Never mind. I'll just pick what looks freshest." I jumped up and sat with Jeannette. "Here, can I just cut up your chicken for you? You need to save your strength to place your bingo chips."

The corners of her mouth lifted just a little.

I bounced back over to be with Marlene and Fred and told Cole about bingo.

"That sounds like fun, eh Grandma? Let's you and me play too." His grandmother looked blankly back at him.

Bingo was being held in the crafts room on the second floor, where we had decorated the Christmas trees. We walked slowly, pushing Helen's wheelchair and allowing Jeannette to shuffle alongside. It took a long time just to get to the elevator. The elevator stayed open an extra moment after we moved on board, programmed I guess to allow seniors to make it in at their pace. Going up was the fastest part of the trip. Then trudge, roll, trudge, we finally made it to the room.

A smiling woman stood near the counter, holding a wire-cylinder basket full of white numbered balls. Three banquet tables took up most of the room. Two were full of seniors already, eight at each. A couple of the women had little strange-haired troll dolls standing near their cards. Another had a little ceramic pig. Cole and I sat at the third table with just Jeannette and Helen, which turned out to be a good thing.

I went to get some cards and markers for Jeannette and Helen from our volunteer bingo caller at the front. From somewhere I remembered that most people play with more than one card. At the other table the ladies seemed to all have four.

Could we handle that many, I mean Cole and I, if we had to do all the playing over their shoulders? I counted out eight.

I returned to the table with the cards and put them on the table in front of Helen and Jeannette. "Don't give me those. They're not lucky. Give me the top four," Jeannette snapped at me.

I quickly scooped the four away from Helen who wouldn't care and exchanged them for the bottom ones. "Here you go. Now you'll win for sure."

"Green daubers are no good. Go back and get hot pink," she commanded.

I smiled at Cole as I returned to the counter and found the pink ones. It was great to see some of Jeannette's spirit returning, even if it was her bossy side.

The volunteer caller at the front sent the metal basket spinning and then pulled out a white ball. "B12. That's B12." The volunteer also printed out the letter and number on the blackboard on the wall.

I scanned Jeannette's cards as quickly as I could. She was quicker, stamping the B12 on the fourth card. "Bingo!" she called.

A woman at the other table stared at her, annoyed.

"No, no," I said gently. "You need to have a complete row to have a bingo."

Jeannette looked at me as though she was peering through clouds. Her eyes squinted. Then, for a moment, life woke in her eyes again. "Of course it's not a bingo. Silly me."

The caller spun the basket again and then caught a ball, holding it up. "G58. G like in great, five eight."

"Bingo!" Jeannette called again.

Cole grinned at me. This time the volunteer walked over. "That's pretty good. Two out of two. But not quite a bingo. You need a few more numbers here or there." She pointed with her finger.

For a while, Jeannette didn't get any numbers. Puzzled, she kept looking over her four cards.

"Over here, Grandma, look. I30." Cole moved his grandmother's hand to the spot and pushed at it gently so the marker stamped the number.

After about a half an hour, someone from the other table called bingo. The caller ran over to check and it turned out to be a legitimate full-row bingo.

"Cheater," Jeannette grumbled. "I wanted that prize."

"Me too," I whispered.

We watched as a lady who helped us decorate trees

received her winnings: a box of green-tea body lotion.

"You aren't even playing," Jeannette snarled at me.

"Yes, but I like green-tea lotion. It's refreshing and smells nice." I headed for the counter.

"Bring back six cards this time," Jeannette commanded. I did as she asked.

I also called my mother on my cell to tell her I would be late.

"You're not with that boy," my mother said.

"No, I'm at the Manor. Do you want me to put the bingo caller on to confirm?"

"No, that's fine. I will save you some supper. You must be starving."

Apology accepted. "Thanks, Mom. See you later."

We played another six rounds. We came close but never scored a full line. Helen Demers won a nightlight for her room. On the other table they won a stuffed animal, a book, some more body lotion, cologne, crocheted slippers, and a mug.

Jeannette eyed the cologne fiercely.

I jumped up and whispered into the caller's ear.

"But we don't have any more prizes."

"Never mind, could you just call N35?" I slipped the volunteer my new plum lipstick still in its package. "And give her this when she wins?"

She nodded, smiled, and touched my shoulder. Then she spun the basket, picked out a ball and called the last number Jeannette needed to win her only real bingo that evening.

"N35!"

"Bingo!" Jeannette called. "Bingo, bingo, bingo!" She stood up and turned to the other tables, holding up her card and grinning.

The caller awarded her my lipstick.

"Can you put some on me, my dear?" She smiled as I opened the package and rolled the plum shade over her lips.

"What a great time," Cole said as we left the crafts room. He leaned over and whispered into my ear. "You are the best." He kissed my cheek while he was there.

That touch of his lips made my heart flip-flop. I had to stop myself from kissing him back more.

Instead, with my face feeling warm, I walked alongside of Jeannette. *Shuffle, shuffle, shuffle.* Cole pushed his grandmother's wheelchair ahead of us. Jeannette became slower as we went. *Shuffle, shuffle,* into the elevator. *Swish,* and down. Out, *shuffle.* I had to nudge her to move over the opening of the door. No smile on her face anymore; her eyes looked vacant again. I took her hand, and led her through the foyer to the lockup — Cole keyed in the code — through the door, just as slow as a herd of snails. Two lipsticks down, but I had been able to make Jeannette happy without putting anyone else in a coma. At least for a moment, which is all an Alzheimer's patient ever gets. I was starving by now, too, but that was okay 'cause both Cole and I were blowing this joint. "Goodbye, Jeannette. Take care, Helen."

Then Mrs. Johnson stuck her head out of the nurse's station. "There's something I need to speak to you about. Can you step in for a moment, Sonja?" Did she want to compliment me on how I was helping Jeannette today? Something in her tone told me not. But what could I have possibly done wrong?

chapter eighteen

The next morning we're back in court and the Crown buzzard asks his most important witness to the stand: Mrs. Johnson, the one who had me charged. She looks a bit older than usual with that tired expression around her eyes. She's put too much concealer around them and the raccoon look really doesn't help. Her honey brown hair appears darker, no slivers of gold in it. I bet she coloured it herself. The top is less poufy today. And the flatness of her dark hair just makes the angles of her face sharper, the wrinkles deeper. She looks tired and angry.

She states her name and occupation and swears on a Bible.

The jury settles in as the buzzard flips through some papers and frowns. The lady who usually wears track suits has a ruffled blue blouse on today and black jeans. The guy in the plaid with jeans has switched to a burgundy shirt and dark pants. The chubby dude wears much more slimming vertical stripes with grey slacks. Even the bearded duo in the back look a bit fresher. Did they all go shopping?

Maybe there's hope for me. I wore a dark-blue shirt paired with black pants. A somber look. I need them to believe

I'm responsible and that I tell the truth.

The buzzard finally speaks. "How would you describe Sonja Ehret's attitude to her volunteer duties at Paradise Manor?"

"Oh, she was just like the rest of the kids who are forced into it by their high school. Sonja did not want to be there. She made up that story about the sewer exploding to cover cutting the first time. The reason she started showing up again was so she could flirt with Cole Demers."

"Objection, Your Honour. The witness cannot possibly know for certain what Sonja's real reason for coming back was."

"Sustained," the judge answers.

Besides, I came back before I even knew Cole.

The buzzard's beak twitches a bit, but he continues. "What was her treatment of the seniors like?"

"That was the only good point about her. Even though she was always screwing up, I didn't kick her out of the program because she was kind to the older people. They seemed to like her a lot, too."

"What do you mean by . . ." the Crown prosecutor makes his fingers into quotation marks, "screwing up?"

"There was the hair dyeing thing with Mrs. Demers and worse, the box of doughnuts Sunny left behind that put Mrs. Demers into a coma. She just generally didn't pay attention to the rules."

"What rules?"

"She didn't like signing in and out, or sanitizing her hands. She wouldn't wait to have new clothes for the residents labelled. She didn't bother about their diet restrictions. Oh, and she really wasn't supposed to be alone in their rooms without supervision. She violated that rule all the time. Most importantly on that last visit on February 14."

"Why did Cole volunteer at the residence? Was he qualifying for his high school requirement too?"

"No, he fulfilled that ages ago. He was just a nice boy who really had a close relationship to his grandmother."

"Would he do things for her?"

"All the time. When she could still walk, he used to take her down the street to the hotel diner for lunch. When she got worse, he brought her things. Magazines. Stuffed animals."

"Would you say he would do anything for her?"

"Absolutely. So when his grandmother wanted her hair done in that silly shade, I do understand why he went along with Sunny."

Went along with Sunny? That is so unfair, he begged me to do it!

"Did you know about his routine of slipping his grandmother a candy at the end of every visit?'

The juror in ruffles sits forward. She's on the edge of her seat. "No. I didn't know anything about it."

How could she not know? That just goes to show you how much adults liked Cole.

"When Mrs. Demers was first admitted, what was her attitude to being in longterm care?"

"She was extremely upset. She didn't want to have to rely on anyone. She said she wanted to die."

The buzzard nods and looks thoughtful.

In the back row of jurors, the guys with goatees shuffle in their seats. One scratches his beard. The man with the crooked glasses eyes him. How can what Helen Demers said be held against me?

"Did anyone else but you hear Helen's wishes?"

"Oh, yes. She repeated it to anyone who would listen. Dr. Lisker, Gillian Halliday, all the staff . . ."

"Cole?" The buzzard flips a page of his notes and appears to be studying them.

"Yes, she told Cole and I know he was troubled about it. He asked me if she was in pain and how long she could be expected to live."

"And how did you answer?" He looks up again.

"That she would never be in any pain in our care and that with routines, proper medication, and good nutrition her memory might make a little recovery."

"How did he react to your answer?"

"Well, he was excited about the prospect of her memory improving. And it did temporarily . . . but then, of course, the disease progressed."

The buzzard nodded and then flipped through his binder. "It says in my notes here that you attended Helen Demers's assessment meeting last year?"

"Yes I did."

"Besides any staff of Paradise Manor, who else attended?"

"Dr. Lisker, Helen's daughter-in-law . . ."

"Was Cole there?"

"Yes. He was so involved with his grandmother, I suggested to his mother that he should attend."

I close my eyes tightly. They're burning from lack of sleep. How can they turn Cole's attention to his grandmother against me? This is so unfair.

"What is typically discussed in such a meeting?"

"Any concerns the primary caregivers might have, medications, progression, special treatments."

"Did any particular questions come up during this meeting?"

"Yes. Dr. Lisker asked Cole's mother if she wanted to sign for palliative care only."

"Meaning what, exactly?"

"Meaning that if Helen Demers became ill she would be made to feel comfortable but she would not be administered any antibiotics or other measures, such as feeding tubes or CPR, to prolong her life."

"Did she agree to sign?"

"No, and Cole argued with her. He told her it was the right thing to do. That his grandmother would have wanted her to sign. That his grandmother wanted to die now."

"Do you feel he had a private agreement with his grandmother to assist in her suicide?"

My lawyer jumps up. "Objection! Leading the witness, Your Honour."

"Sustained."

Heh, heh, the man formerly in plaid coughs. The bearded guy with all the piercings leans forward.

"Mrs. Johnson, do you know what time Sunny left on February 14?"

"Yes, I do. She didn't sign out that day but that's not unusual for Sunny. I happened to be heading towards the recreation room when I saw her leave Mrs. Demers's room. It was five-thirty."

"And when was Mrs. Demers's death discovered?"

"Five-forty when one of the attendants went to feed her. Sunny Ehret was the last person to see Helen Demers alive."

The Eighteenth Visit — four hours left

Isn't it great, Mr. Brooks? Even Alzheimer's patients can find true romance at Paradise Manor. Fred and Marlene, two residents, started walking together and one thing led to another. Now they're in love. Meanwhile, I'm helping Mrs. Johnson keep track of some of the patients' personal items. I'm good with these old people, I can help them remember what they did with their stuff.

The nursing station was empty except for Mrs. Johnson, who stood waiting for me. "Close the door behind you, please."

If she wasn't taking a seat neither would I. I didn't want her towering over me. She lifted the front of her hair with her fingers. Nervous, fidgety. Why? She called me in, after all. She had all the power. She opened her mouth, shut it, and then opened it again and just started talking at me. "Jeannette Ferrier's niece was in yesterday and she wanted to know where her thirty-year service pin went. You didn't happen to see it, did you?"

"I don't remember any pin. Did you check in the shower room? You know they have a stack of glasses there from when they forget to return them to the residents' faces."

Mrs. Johnson's mouth pulled down out of shape. "No." A sour note, like I'd insulted her, "Jeannette doesn't wear this pin. It's usually on the photo of her in her room, pinned to the frame."

"Oh, yeah? What does it look like? Maybe I'll see one of the other residents wearing it."

"It's ten-carat gold and about this size," she touched her pointer finger to her thumb. "A miniature camera and where the lens would be is a diamond."

"Whoa, that sounds valuable. Oh, ohhh. You think I took it!"

"I didn't say that. I just asked you because she likes you a lot. Maybe she even gave it to you, for all I know." She tucked some of her hair behind her ear.

"I wouldn't accept a present like that without checking with you."

She untucked her hair again. "Good. That's very good, in fact. Other things have been disappearing, too. Marlene's gold earrings, Evelyn's wedding band . . ." Evelyn was the new lady who had taken Susan's room.

"But that's awful. Who would take such personal stuff? I mean, those things have so much sentimental value."

"I don't know. Maybe you can let me know if you see one of the residents wandering into other rooms. Or if you see a visitor, that biker or anyone . . ."

Donny. It came to me in a flash. Was that who she was thinking about too? Could he sink that low? It was all a game for him. Was there any challenge to lifting things from Alzheimer's patients?

"I'll watch for that pin. I just hope it didn't get vacuumed up or something."

Mrs. Johnson shook her head. "I certainly hope it turns up again."

"Good night, Mrs. Johnson. See you next week." I left the nursing station. Cole had waited for me and I told him about the missing things. "How come she didn't call you in to discuss them with you?"

"Well, if she's mostly looking for that camera pin, it makes sense. You know Jeannette better than I do. You give her stuff, she might want to give you something back. Grandma used to insist I take spare rolls of toilet paper back with me."

"What did you do?"

"Well, she got pretty upset if I didn't. So I took the toilet paper and just returned it at reception. How's Donovan?"

"He's fine. Why do you ask?" I squinted at him. "He doesn't need some old lady's service pin."

"Geez, I wasn't thinking about him stealing. I just hoped you'd broken up with him. Does he have a gambling addiction or anything?"

I rolled my eyes at Cole. "No. And I haven't broken up with him."

"The dance is the weekend after Valentine's Day." He reached into a jean pocket and pulled out a couple of long stubs of cardboard. "I bought two tickets betting you couldn't last till then with that jerk."

"He's not a jerk, Cole." But everyone did have me wondering about him. His shoplifting, that was kind of a gambling addiction when you thought about it. My cell went off and I read Donny's text message.

Where r u?

The Manor, I texted back.

Can pick u up

Pls do

"You coming to the bus?" Cole asked when I flipped the phone shut.

"No, Donovan's giving me a ride."

"Well, okay. I'll see you. You've got four hours left, right?"

"Right, two visits, four hours."

"Still time to change your mind. Bye!" The bus approached from around the bend and Cole began running for the stop. When he was almost there, his feet slipped out from under him and he fell spectacularly. "I'm okay." He waved at me from the sidewalk.

I shook my head. That kind of thing didn't happen to Donny. He wouldn't take a bus, and he wouldn't run for one. Besides, he was more coordinated and wouldn't go flying like that.

When his car pulled up, I jumped in.

"Hello, Beautiful." He reached over and kissed me. "Where to?"

"Take me to the Princess building, only let me off before the turn."

"Sure." He drove out from the paved circle in front of the Manor, onto the parking lot road, and then out to the street. It was wintry dark. Within a few moments, we passed Cole's bus, lit up brightly against that dark. I saw his face. He was watching the car, which stood out because of its strange bitter-orange colour. Tango, Donny told me it was called. His father had paid extra for the shade, which meant no one owned one like it. I waved at Cole, but I didn't think he saw me. It was too dark and we were ahead of the bus by then. He looked kind of sad.

"Donny, you didn't take something from Jeannette's room, did you?"

His eyes stayed on the road even as we stopped for a red light. "Jeannette who?" he asked without turning to face me.

"That lady from Paradise Manor."

"Sunny, there are so many old ladies. How can anyone remember them all?"

"Did you take something from any of their rooms? Jewellery, you know, or maybe a pin with a diamond?" I stared at the side of his face, looking for a reaction, embarrassment or anger.

He seemed to sit up straighter. His neck stiffened and he lifted his chin. "Your questions are really insulting, you know?"

I brushed a curl from his cheek, and saw the hurt in the smoke of his eyes. "I'm sorry, you're right." I sighed. "Mrs. Johnson just finished grilling me. I shouldn't have done the same thing to you."

"Yeah. 'Cause you told me none of their junk was valuable, so why would I bother? Maybe your pal Cole lifted some stuff. He probably has a whole operation going there."

"Oh, come on." I shook my head. We drove another five blocks and then turned onto the street where my parents' condos were. He slowed down. "You know what, it's cold out. Just take me up to the front door. My parents are never going to notice."

Of course Donovan lingered at the front door, leaning over, kissing me. I held him. It felt good; his strong body close to mine. So good-looking, so gallant to the ladies at Paradise Manor. He really was the perfect guy. I'd had no right to feel suspicious. Why do people always suspect you when you do something nice?

So the next visit to Paradise Manor, I decided to really look for those missing items. I checked in the shower room and found a St. Christopher's medal on a chain. The nurse said it belonged to the new guy. She explained he was in here because of a brain injury in a biking accident. "You'd think he would try and keep track of his saint!" She chuckled.

I returned it to his room and while I was there, I looked around for any trinkets. Nothing. As I stepped out, I noticed Mrs. Johnson giving me the evil eye. But you can't really defend yourself against a look, can you? If I said something like, "I wasn't doing anything wrong, just a favour for one of the nurses," wouldn't that sound like I had a guilty conscience or something?

I headed back to the dining room so I could help feed the old people.

Jeannette called to me. "Lovely coat you have there."

I was actually still wearing one; I hadn't taken it off yet. It was one of those poufy white ski jackets that made it look like I was wearing a bunch of marshmallows sewn together. "Thanks, Jeannette. You're looking very good yourself." Honestly, though, her grey hair was slicked back behind her ears and it was kind of oily-looking. A little white lie. "Can I ask you, Jeannette, did you give anybody a present lately?"

"No, how could I? There are no stores, I don't have any of my own money." Her eyes lit up. "Ah, but did you know Fred asked Marlene to marry him?"

"Really. That's very surprising. You know he's married to someone else."

Jeannette's lively brown eyes seemed to dull over as I told her. I had spoiled a fairy-tale romance for her, I suppose. How could I have been that mean?

"Why don't we go to supper together?" I suggested. I helped her stand up and attach herself to her walker. Then we crept along, so slowly it was hard to tell we were moving. Finally I stepped around Jeannette so I could open the door to the dining room.

I waved to Cole who was already grabbing a tray for his grandmother. He smiled.

I helped Jeannette settle in and then ran back to open the door for Fred and Marlene so they didn't have to drop their handholding to get in.

I guided the two of them to their seats near Jeannette.

Once they sat down and had their chicken and rice in front of them, they seemed to have a hard time parting their hands.

"Just for now." I gently pried Fred's fingers from around Marlene's.

"We're married, you know," Marlene told me.

"So soon? I just heard you got engaged." I looked down at her hand as though looking for an engagement ring. That's when I noticed something weird. She was wearing two gold bands.

chapter nineteen

"Does the defence wish to question the witness?"

"Thank you, Your Honour, yes." My lawyer stands and pauses for a moment, not looking at any notes, just staring at Mrs. Johnson. "Do you enjoy working with young people?"

"I'm not sure I understand what you mean." Mrs. Johnson lifts the front of her hair with her fingers. Fidgety. "Obviously my line of work is with seniors."

Michael clears his throat. "Let me rephrase the question. You said earlier that Sonja was like most high school volunteers, that she didn't want to be there. How do you work with that kind of arrangement? Do you have to be on top of the volunteers all the time, to make sure they do everything and make sure they do it right?"

"I'm too busy to be directly involved. Gillian Halliday supervises the students. We need volunteers. The seniors benefit from the extra social contact."

"If you were not directly involved, how did you know that Sonja was 'screwing up' so much, as you told the court earlier?"

Mrs. Johnson's lip twitches now. I've never seen it do that before.

"Because of the effects. If Helen Demers hadn't had ridiculous hair, I wouldn't have known about Sonja dyeing it without consent. If Helen hadn't gone into a coma, I wouldn't have known that Sonja had fed her a box of doughnuts."

"But you knew about Sonja not wanting to wash her hands or label clothing."

She pulls at her hair again. "I did watch her a little more closely because she missed her first appointment with us and was on probation."

"Was she on probation because she said that Paradise Manor smelled bad?"

Mrs. Johnson turns bright red. "We do the best we can with the seniors. We change them frequently. Our home was voted number one in *The Post*. We have an excellent reputation."

"But Sonja didn't make that first appointment because she thought a sewer had exploded. That annoyed you, didn't it?"

"Sonja Ehret is a liar. She never seriously believed we were evacuating the residents due to a broken sewage pipe."

From behind me, I hear my mother call Mrs. Johnson a witch under her breath. I sigh. *Angry is better than ashamed,* I think.

"But there was an odour in the foyer. She couldn't take the smell. Have you had other volunteers resign because of the odour?"

Mrs. Johnson turns to the judge, eyes watering, skin the colour of a deep sunburn.

"Answer the question, please," he tells her.

"Yes."

"You are the one who initiated the charges against

Sonja Ehret, are you not?"

"Yes, but I did it on behalf of the Manor."

"You told this court that Paradise Manor has an exceptional reputation in the community. How did you fare on your last Compliance Review?"

The red in her face breaks up. Is she getting hives? She sits up straighter. Her neck gets longer. She blinks a few times. "We were cited for two unmet standards. But one was for not reporting properly on incidents during a very busy time and we've rectified the situation."

"And the other?"

She waits a few moments. "A resident did not get cleaned up quickly enough." She pounds the desk in front of her and raises her voice. "But it was during a flu epidemic."

Heh, heh, the juror in the front row coughs.

Michael speaks calmly. "You didn't really like Sonja Ehret, did you?"

"My liking her had nothing to do with this."

"She said Paradise Manor stank. She wore coffee beans around her neck so she could stand the smell."

"She's a spoiled brat," Mrs. Johnson hisses.

"Would a spoiled brat commit manslaughter?" Michael snaps back.

"She did whatever she felt like," Mrs. Johnson said. "There was never any stopping her."

"Really? But you and your staff were too busy to report incidents and clean residents in a timely fashion. Weren't you also too busy to check on Helen Demers on February 14?"

"No, no!" Mrs. Johnson slams her hands on the desk in front of her.

"You said yourself Sonja left at five-thirty. That it was ten minutes before someone else looked in on Helen Demers."

"But it was Sonja's fault. She shouldn't have given her the candy!"

"Isn't it true that if someone had just looked in a few minutes earlier, the Heimlich manoeuvre could have saved Mrs. Demers?"

"Yes, but —"

"Isn't it also true that you never saw Sonja give a candy to Mrs. Demers?"

Mrs. Johnson's face flushes a deep red. "Yes, I didn't see it personally, but —"

"No further questions."

The buzzard rises quickly to his feet. "Your Honour, I would like to request that court adjourn for an early lunch. The Crown wishes to discuss something with the defence."

The judge looks at his watch and frowns. "It's eleven-thirty now. Let us adjourn till two. Will that give you enough time, Mr. Dougal?"

"Yes, Your Honour."

"So be it then." He stands.

"All rise," the court clerk announces. The jury and people in the court stand, too. There aren't many people. My parents and I wait with Michael McCann. The judge and jury leave the courtroom and the buzzard approaches us.

"Why don't you wait for me in the cafeteria? Mr. Dougal and I need to talk alone first," Michael says.

My father nods and we shuffle out, down the hall to the bland little room with a soft-drink machine in one corner and a square window hole near another. A lady in an apron toasts bagels and pours coffee behind that square.

"Do you want something?" my father asks my mother.

"A coffee would be nice."

"Sunny?" He raises his eyebrows at me.

I shake my head and Mom frowns at me. I've lost ten pounds since last year, big deal. "Okay fine, a strawberry yogurt, please."

He orders and we sit at the table, waiting. Dad brings over the coffee and my yogurt. Then he returns to the window for a couple of warmed cranberry lemon muffins. He brings those back to the table, too, and slices each in half with one of those white plastic knives. "Here. Take a piece. You too." He looks at my mother.

There's always a gnawing in my stomach. I have no idea if I'm ever hungry anymore. I take a spoonful of yogurt and try to taste the smooth tartness. Mom takes one piece of the muffin and nudges the plate towards me.

I take a piece. I think it's good, sour and sweet like the yogurt.

"What do you think that lawyer wants to talk to Michael about?"

"Who knows," Dad answers. "But we're about to find out." He nods his head towards the entrance.

Michael McCann passes through the door to the lunch-room and approaches. His lips play a little half smile as he sits down. He sighs. "Good news. The Crown is offering leniency again."

"You mean if I plead guilty now, I won't have to go away?" I ask, smiling.

"Yes. Mr. Dougal will recommend that you get community service."

"But this means he thinks he will lose, yes?" my mother asks. "Why should Sunny plead guilty if we are going to win?"

"Because everything depends on what the jury decides," Michael says. "No one can really predict what they will decide."

"Do we really want to rely on them for my whole future?" I ask her.

Mom tilts her head. "Will she have a record?"

Mr. McCann nods. "In a few years we can ask to have it sealed, though."

"What does sealed mean?" she asks.

"It doesn't matter, Mom. I want to change my plea. I can't risk going away from you right now."

"Yes, it matters. The doctor will say I'm sick or not Thursday morning. You will have this record, regardless."

"Sealed means if someone searches your name for charges, the charge will no longer show up."

"When she applies for a job, she can say she doesn't have a record?" my father asks.

Mr. McCann's mouth crumples into a frown. "If she's asked whether she's ever committed a crime, then the truthful answer is still yes. But if she says no, I would say there is no way for the potential employer to find out."

So in a few years, I can lie my way into an apprenticeship at Salon Teo. Will the details even matter to me then if Mom is dead? I sigh.

"Can I still have the record sealed if I'm convicted?"

"Yes."

"So what do you think we should do?" my father asks.

My lawyer shakes his head. "We have a strong case. I'd like to say I'm sure we can win. But I can't be certain. It's your call."

That jury — what did it really think about me? I look at

my mother, who purses her lips. Only a small cross of wrinkles separates her brows. My father puts his hand over hers. This could all be over right now if I just say yes, I'm guilty. They could go back to their business at the condo. They wouldn't have to keep paying this lawyer or enduring this trial.

And if I don't plead guilty but the jury decides I am anyway, I would spend two years in a young offenders' institute. I wouldn't be there for Mom for her next treatments if there even are any. I blink back tears.

It's too much to risk. I look at the ceiling.

"Sunny, don't do this thing," my mother tells me.

I shake my head and chew my lip. I look at my lawyer.

"Whatever you decide." He shrugs his shoulders.

My mother seems so sure.

I shake my head at her. "Fine. We'll continue with the trial."

My mother smiles.

The Nineteenth Visit — two hours left

Did Mrs. Johnson tell you that I found Marlene's missing gold wedding band? Also I'm on the lookout for Jeannette's service pin. The staff has to appreciate my efforts and I know you'll give me A, Mr. Brooks, because I deserve it.

Monday morning when I grabbed a pair of panties from my top drawer, something pricked at my finger. So that was where my amethyst earring went! Yah! My jewellery box sits on my dresser just above my lingerie drawer, so I guess it must have fallen in from there. Now I had the pair together again. Grinning, I quickly put them on. Finding them had also given me an idea about Jeannette's missing service pin. I wasn't sure where the framed picture of her hung — I mean the one that the camera pin had been stuck to — but I would search any drawers directly beneath it. After school that day, I could hardly wait to get to Paradise Manor. I was so sure about my theory.

"Hi, Katherine. How are you?" I called as I signed in.

"Fine. Nice earrings."

"Thanks. My grandmother gave them to me." I made a production of sanitizing my hands, spreading my good mood and goodwill to all. "See you later." I saluted her as I breezed over to lockup. The code worked first try and I walked towards Jeannette's room.

"How are you, Gorgeous?"

I stopped when I heard her voice. "Great, Jeannette. I have an idea where your camera pin went. Want to come with me to look?"

Her eyes went blank and her face turned slack. She didn't say anything.

I put my own face close to hers, trying to bring her back to this planet. "Your room. I'm going to your room. Want to come with me?"

Still no answer.

"Okay, well I'll see you in the dining room in a few minutes." I kept walking, said hello to that new care worker on the way, and then turned and walked through the open door to Jeannette's room. Aha! Just as I thought, there was a dresser directly underneath the photo and the top drawer was even open. It was just a crack, but enough for a small piece of jewellery to pass through.

I slid it open but there were hygiene products in there,

not clothes — some moisturizer, a brush, a tensor bandage. I lifted each out, one by one, confident that underneath some article I would find that service pin.

"What are you doing?" Mrs. Johnson snapped from behind me.

I jumped. "I . . . I was looking for that missing camera pin. You see, this morning . . ."

Ever notice that the more you explain, the lamer you sound? This was especially true now, 'cause Mrs. Johnson made me nervous anyway. "I found this earring that I thought I had lost forever right in my lingerie." I showed her my amethyst earrings as though that would prove anything.

"You are not to go into any of the residents' rooms alone. Do you understand me?" Mrs. Johnson didn't yell, but her message came out crisp as a rice cake.

"Sure. But if you don't want me to look, could you just take a peek yourself. Make sure it didn't fall in there?"

She rolled her eyes and pointed to the door. Clearly finding that brooch wasn't top priority for her. I headed for the dining room, feeling like I'd been slapped in the face.

Later, when I told Alexis about it on the phone, she tried to cheer me up. "Don't you think finding your grandma's earring was like a message from her? Like everything's okay, don't worry?"

I touched my earlobes. "You're right. I feel really good about having the pair together again. Like I've won a contest. Maybe it was Omi talking to me."

"And you know what? Your next visit to the home will be the last two hours you ever have to spend there. Don't worry about what Mrs. Johnson thinks. You'll never have to deal with her again."

"Hmm. I'll miss some of the old people." And Cole. I could keep him as a Monday friend as long as I volunteered there. Once I left, I had to decide: did I lose him entirely or did he become something more?

Alexis seemed to realize that she'd hit an underbelly. "I know! Let's do some retail therapy, this weekend. Just you and me."

I pumped enthusiasm into my voice. "Girl's day at the mall. I like it."

"We'll have iced lattes!"

"In February. It will be great."

So that's where we headed Saturday afternoon. The stores had their formal wear for the spring season out already. Perfect. We browsed the stores saving our favourite, the Patches boutique, for last. Alexis pulled a great white prom dress off a rack. "With your dark hair and your complexion, this would really go well."

I winced at it. "Too much like a wedding dress."

"Really? It's a winter white." She held it up to me.

"Yeah, and Donny's grad is in the spring." I saw myself in the mirror. The colour did look good against my skin. Alexis had a great eye for shopping. "Did I tell you about the wedding we had at the old-age home?" I asked her as I handed back the dress.

"No. C'mon, you did not!" She hung it back up again.

"Oh yes, we did. You know Fred and Marlene, and how they're always walking together?"

"That sweet couple you told me about?" Alexis pulled out a ruby red dress.

"Alexis, that screams Valentine's Day." She shrugged and I took the dress for a moment. *Cole's dance.* Nah, too formal.

Besides I wasn't going. I hung it back up. "Yeah, so Fred gave Marlene a wedding band. But the ring belonged to Evelyn, the new patient who got Susan's room after she died."

"He stole it from her?"

"We don't know. How would Fred have gotten the ring off Evelyn's finger? Maybe she gave it to him. Or she took it off to wash her hands and he just picked it up. It's not like we can get clear answers out of her, or him for that matter. Mrs. Johnson practically accused me of taking it so when I saw two rings on Marlene's finger I had to report it to Gillian Halliday."

"What did she do?" Alexis pulled out a black dress which would have looked knock-em-dead on her.

"She tried to coax it away from Marlene but instead of giving it back the poor thing burst into tears."

"Aw." Alexis held the black dress against herself.

"We're shopping for me here."

She quickly hung it back on the rack.

I pulled it out again and held it against me. "What do you think? Too dark?"

"No, I think those pink streaks in your hair make it all work. Still, if it's for a spring prom . . . How about this?" She held out a shimmery blue number with a single shoulder strap on a diagonal.

"Maybe I'll try that one on." I took it into my hands.

"So how did you get the ring from Marlene?"

"Oh, I traded her for the cubic zirconia Donny gave me. It's way more sparkly so she liked that. And Cole told her he would perform an actual ceremony."

Alexis wrinkled her nose. "Is that even legal?"

I rolled my eyes at her. "They're both married to other people. And Cole isn't even an Internet priest. Still it made her happy for a little while and, of course, Mrs. Johnson was off that day. We gathered up a group of the seniors in the television room and borrowed a bouquet of plastic flowers from the foyer upstairs. And Cole got them to recite some vows."

"Just like we used to do in kindergarten at recess."

"Oh yeah, that's true. We used to play marriage." I thought for a moment about how the seniors' lives seemed to be replaying backwards. "Except in the middle of this ceremony, Marlene decided they needed to go to the store for some bread before it closed."

"Wow. Did that hurt Fred's feelings?" she asked as she flipped back dresses. "Here's another one that could work. It's bright."

"Nah, they just walked off hand in hand." I looked at the dress she had separated from the rest. "This is lime, Alexis! You think I want to wear lime to the prom?"

She shrugged. "It's kiwi, not lime. And it makes a statement."

I took it, along with the blue dress, into the changing room.

"What's Donny going to say when he hears you've given away his ring?" Alexis said a few minutes later, just as I slid the blue dress over my head and onto my body.

I gasped when I looked in the mirror. That single bare shoulder looked dramatic against the shimmer. I just had to have that dress. And I needed to wear it to Donny's grad.

"Sunny? Can I see?"

I opened the door.

She nodded. "Mmm hmm. That one's really you." She just stared for a second. "You're not even going to tell Donovan about the ring, are you?"

"Lexie, of course I am. I'll just say I lost it somewhere at the Manor."

Alexis fumbled for the price tag on the dress. "One hundred and twenty dollars. That's not bad. But is your Mom going to pay for a dress that you're wearing to Donny's grad?"

I frowned. "No. I'll just have to figure out another way. You don't have any money, do you?"

She made a face. "Five dollars. Would that be enough for them to hold it for you?" she asked.

I shrugged.

"You know, there's a couple in your size. Maybe they'll go on sale later in the season."

The salesclerk walked over to us. "That looks stunning on you. Is there anything I can help you with?"

"Can you hold this dress for us? I don't have the money right now. But I only need it in April anyway."

"I could keep it aside till the end of the day," she suggested hopefully. "But I can't put it away any longer and at that price, well . . . " She shook her head.

"That does it. I'm texting Donovan. We need a lift home anyway." I took my cell phone from my purse and keyed in: *Found perfect dress. Need money. Meet me @ food court?* I put the phone back in my purse and talked to the salesclerk again. "Yes, if you could hold it till closing for me that would be great." I changed back into my clothes and handed the dress to her.

Then we walked towards the south side of the mall where all the noise and food smells came from. At the coffee shop, we decided the ice lattes would be way too fattening. My phone buzzed just as I ordered a Chai tea. *OK,* Donovan texted me back.

"Where's he going to get the money? He's not going to steal it, is he Sunny?" Alexis hissed as she looked over my shoulder.

"No!" I shook my head at her. We grabbed our teas, added some sugar, and headed for a table with four chairs. "For your information, Donovan isn't always broke. Maybe he has some Christmas money left." *Oh right, in February.* Even I knew how unlikely that would be. "I just wish I could have volunteered at Salon Teo. The tips alone probably would have covered the dress."

"Come on, you said it yourself before, you love those old people," Alexis said.

"You're right. I do. I just want to be able to buy things for myself." I sipped at my tea and tried to relax. But a grabby feeling inside made me tense. *That dress, that perfect shimmering one-shouldered dress.* My life wouldn't be the same without it.

To take my mind off things, Alexis told me her volunteer story about a Jack Russell puppy the shelter adopted out on Friday. *Yada, yada, yada.* Alexis was all about giving out lots of details. Apparently people buy the dogs without realizing how much energy they have. Then they dump them. They're really difficult to place but Alexis's photo of the dog on their website drew some dog lovers in.

"Here, let me show you his picture." She held out her cell phone to me. The dog's hair stuck up in the middle, which reminded me of something.

"Why is he so shaggy?" I asked, pointing to the fluff in the middle of his head.

"We think he has some poodle in him."

"Cole," I said out loud. That's who that fluff reminded me of. Even as I said his name I saw Donovan heading towards us.

He was confident, cool. His curls were glossy and his brown eyes soulful. He looked very Johnny Depp. I felt my face open into a grin. I took a last look at the Cole puppy and snapped Alexis's phone shut. "He's very cute."

"Hey, Sunny. Alexis, nice to see you," Donny called from two tables away.

"Hi, Donovan," she answered back.

One more table and I stood up to give him a squeeze. "Thanks for coming, Donny." I kissed him quickly on the mouth, not long enough to embarrass Alexis and not short enough to be cold to him.

"Anytime and always, Beautiful." He sat down with us. "So you found something special, did you?"

"Yeah, it's light blue with a hint of shine to it in a certain light. The strap comes down like this." I made a motion with my hand. "Do you want to come see it?"

"I don't need to, Sunny. The way you talk about it, I know you love it. That's enough for me." He took his wallet from his pocket. "What do you need?" He pulled out a few bills.

"You don't have enough, do you? It will be about a hundred and thirty with tax." I reached hesitantly just as a receipt dropped down.

He made a grab for it but my hand was closer. I was about to hand it back to him only something made me unfold it instead. Murphy's Pawnshop. My face blazed when I made out two scribbled words: gold pin. "How did you get the money, Donovan?" I held up the receipt. I wasn't really asking, 'cause I already knew.

"Hey, leave that. I said take the money, not go through my stuff."

"Yeah, but it sure seems like you go through other

people's stuff." I frowned, looking at the twenty-dollar bills and the receipt. My cheeks steamed. I wanted to hit Donovan so badly. "Well, you know what?" I stacked them up along with the receipt and put them in the zipped part of my purse. "This money is going back to the pawnshop. I'm getting Jeannette Ferrier's thirty-year service pin."

"Is that what that thing was? I found it on the floor. I asked the old lady if it was hers. She didn't seem to recognize it."

I looked at his face. I wanted to believe him. "But I asked you if you took anything from anyone's room and you told me no." His smoky eyes didn't look so dreamy anymore, they looked like they were trying to find an escape somewhere.

"'Cause I didn't take it," he insisted.

"Have it your way. But now that you know, we have to do the right thing. Can you drive us there?"

"But, Sunny, she'll never know the difference." Donovan threw up his hands in a panic. "And you won't get your dress for the prom."

"At this point, I'm not sure I even want to go to your grad."

chapter twenty

"You're absolutely sure about continuing with this," Michael McCann asks before we return to the court.

"Yes," I tell him.

"All right then." He breaks into a grin. "Let's go in there and convince them that you're innocent."

The jury comes back happy looking. The chubby dude pats at his gut. Is that soya sauce I see down the sleeveless T-shirt of that lady? There's a Chinese buffet restaurant around the corner. Those twelve jurors will be sleepy and slow just when it's our turn to give my side of the story.

The judge speaks to the Crown lawyer and nods at whatever he says. We all take our places. I sit down in my special box, front row, slightly to the right of the centre of the court.

"Your Honour, I would like to call Patrick Gale to the stand."

The prosecuting buzzard furrows his brows. You can tell he's confused. The Crown is required to give the defence a list of witnesses who will be called to the stand, but defence doesn't have to name theirs. And the name doesn't mean anything to anybody. Not even me — except I know that Michael McCann had his assistant make phone calls to the family of that younger man in Johann's old room. Through her discussions with them she tracked down Patrick.

He lumbers down the aisle, large and scary, even though his tattoos are covered by what looks to be a wrinkle-free shirt. He wears a black leather vest over black jeans. Formal biker wear, I'm guessing.

Patrick Gale swears in on the Bible and states his occupation to be a forklift driver at General Motors. He looks around the courtroom and smiles. Why not? He's not up on any charges. There's no risk for him at all.

"Mr. Gale, can you tell the court how it was that you came to visit Paradise Manor in February of last year?"

"Certainly," he answers in a gravely smoker's voice. "Brother of mine had a motorcycle accident. Bad one, too."

"Excuse me for interrupting. To be clear, when you say brother, do you mean Frank Conner is actually your sibling?"

"Sibling? No." He wags his head. "He was a biking brother. We belonged to the same club."

I see the lady in the ruffled shirt lean far back in her chair. The man dressed in a burgundy shirt and dark pants raises his chin.

"And you said he was hurt badly?"

The biker twirls a finger at his ear. "Not ever going to be right in the head again. So he moved into Paradise Manor and I came for a visit."

"Did you bring anything?"

"Yup. A box of Timmies." He smiles. "Figured it might cheer him up a little."

"Did you leave the box behind?" Michael asks.

I'm nervous about this question. I told Michael about leaving the doughnuts in Jeannette's lap, and the lie I told Mrs.

Johnson. He explained to me that it wouldn't matter what Mr. Gale answered, as long as he introduced some doubt into who caused Mrs. Demers's diabetic coma.

The biker nods. "I didn't see a recycling box but figured the cleaners would know where it was."

"Who ate all the doughnuts? Was it your friend?"

"No, he had one cruller. I handed them out to the rest of the old folk. One old lady must have had about four."

A photo of Mrs. Demers flashes up on the small screen.

"Was this the resident who ate so many doughnuts?"

The biker shrugged his shoulders. "Couldn't tell you for sure. They all look the same to me."

"No further questions."

But he should have been able to tell Helen apart from the others; she had candy cane–coloured hair after all. Not in the photo on the screen though. A little deception on the defence's part.

The judge leans forward. "Does the Crown have any questions for Mr. Gale?"

I hold my breath, wondering if the buzzard picked up on the all-grey hair detail.

"No, Your Honour."

I exhale and can't help smiling as the biker lumbers back out of the courtroom.

The Twentieth Visit — I'm all done

Good news, Mr. Brooks. I found the missing camera brooch and pinned it on Jeannette so she could enjoy it. This was my last compulsory visit to Paradise Manor. In conclusion, as the voluntary requirement states, I understand my role in serving the community and I have a greater sense of belonging. I may still pop into Paradise Manor from time to time, but I wish to pursue a career in hairstyling so will now apply for an internship at Salon Teo.

"I didn't do it. I promise."

When a person keeps saying the same thing over and over, your heart wants to accept the words even if your mind keeps reminding you they can't be true.

"I'll find a way to buy that dress for you," Donovan also promised as we left the pawnshop. He opened the car door for me and Alexis. Then he went to his side and slid in. "They called me for an interview at Pizzalicious. I'll even throw pizza in the air to make dough for you."

In the back seat Alexis chuckled. Traitor.

Donovan looked at me, waiting for something.

I squinted at him. "You know that's not why I'm mad."

"But that dress was gorgeous. You have every reason to be disappointed." He started the engine. "I don't blame you."

So gallant, so honourable . . . What an act. "You took something from Jeannette Ferrier," I hissed. "Donny, she's lost all her memories. You can't rob her of her souvenirs too."

"Well, if you think I stole something from one of the golden geezers, then I'm mad at you. How can you not believe me after seven months together?" He faced towards the road, not looking my way.

I watched his profile — curls softening a hard jawline, smoky brown eyes that could melt you. I didn't believe him because he lied all the time, to his parents and his teachers, to his friends, too. When the truth was inconvenient, when it was uncomfortable, when it meant trouble — if deception smoothed things over, then Donovan lied. Still, I didn't want to think he stole the pin from Jeannette.

"You've got that ugly camera brooch back. What more do you want?" He gave me a quick dark glance.

I looked away and didn't answer, couldn't answer really. Breaking up with Donovan was huge. I loved having him as a boyfriend. No Donovan, no grad dance, no dress. Alexis was my only other friend. I would feel lonely.

"Where's your ring?" he suddenly asked me.

On the defence now, I stumbled. "It . . . um . . . slipped off when I was helping Marlene to her walker. You just reminded me. I'll have to check at the reception desk to see if anyone found it."

Donny turned his head a second time so his eyes could meet mine. One set of lying eyes calling to another set. So I couldn't break up with him just then. We were both guilty.

That Monday I met up with Cole on the bus to the Manor. He wore a crazy court-jester hat that I snatched off his head immediately. I liked the hat; I just needed to see his hair sticking up. It looked honest, puppy-like now that I'd seen Alexis's photo from the pound. "I'm glad you used the bus. It's much safer in this weather."

"Me too, since you're here." He grinned. "I had to make a deal with my mother. Unless the streets are absolutely clear, I will not take the bike."

He was a promise keeper, even if his mother wasn't there to check up on him. I admired that. He reminded me, too, that I did have other people in my life who liked me besides Donovan.

"This is your last volunteer session." His voice wobbled and he turned to rub at the ice on the window. There was a small lookout hole when he finished.

"Yes. But I am thinking of breaking up with Donny."

He turned back to me, a smile stretching across his face.

I showed him Jeannette's brooch and told him what happened. "I need to get it back to her without Mrs. Johnson knowing. Can you help me?"

He agreed to be a lookout for me when I returned the pin to Jeannette.

The bus stopped and he got off first, reaching his hand up to hold me steady as I made the step down to the ice. He didn't let go of my hand as we walked to the Manor. It felt right. I wouldn't fall.

I realized in that moment that being with him felt better than hanging around Donny.

We went through the doors, signed the book, released each other's hands to sanitize them, and then passed into the lockup ward.

We spotted Marlene talking to Mrs. Johnson. She was holding a hand up, showing her my ring. I cringed as we drew nearer and overheard the discussion. "It was a beautiful ceremony. I'm so sorry you couldn't make it."

"Hello, Cole. Sonja," Mrs. Johnson called.

"Hi," I answered.

"Hello," Cole said.

"So you know the minister and his wife?" Marlene asked.

"Yes, I do." Mrs. Johnson's eyes narrowed as she looked at me. Only me. Not Cole, the minister who actually performed the ceremony.

"It was a nice wedding," Cole said as we continued past.

I giggled.

We found his grandmother and Jeannette, conveniently sitting side by side, in the television room. We hung up our coats in the closet and headed over to them.

"What a beautiful smile," Jeannette told me as we drew nearer.

"Thank you," I said and then actually did smile.

"I'll go back to the door and watch for you," Cole told me.

"Thanks." I kneeled down and took the camera pin from my purse.

"This belongs to you, Jeannette. I found it on the floor." I stuck the camera on her collar and bent the pin in to close it.

"Thank you. Such a wonderful present. I can't believe it."

"You deserve it, Jeannette. Thirty years of service, you've earned it."

"But I'm only twenty-nine years old," she answered.

I didn't know what to say back. "Can you keep your present a secret? Just between you and me?"

Her eyes darted side to side, then squinted. I watched the bright light in them fade till they looked vague and faraway.

"Sure I'll help out at the Valentine's party." Cole's voice broadcast extra loud from the corridor. He was warning me. I stood up quickly.

Gillian Halliday breezed into the room, smiling and saying hello to the various residents. Here a shoulder pat, there a hand rub. She got to Jeannette but didn't notice the brooch. "I see you have your favourite visitor," she said to her and then turned to me. "Will you come for the Valentine's party? Cole's already agreed to help out."

"I heard, but my hours are done now."

"Oh my, time goes fast." Her mouth turned down a little. "Still, if you just feel like returnin' on your own, you know I've loved havin' you. And so did the residents. Anytime. Not just Valentine's Day."

I smiled back at her. She made me want to come again.

"Did you see the lovely present the young lady gave me?" Jeannette suddenly broke in, pointing to her pin.

So much for keeping the camera brooch a secret. I felt my skin warm. "We found it on a walker in the hall." That was the fallback story Cole and I had agreed on.

"That's a wonderful present," Gillian said. She touched my hand. "Come back soon." She winked at me. "Time to get them to the dinin' room."

This would be my last time helping Marlene and Fred eat, I thought as we guided our old people to their tables. I watched Fred's hand tremble as he navigated his spoon of potato soup to his mouth. I wanted to hold it steady but I knew it was already hard for him to accept that I cut his meat.

I dabbed some gravy off Marlene's chin. Evelyn didn't like her meatloaf so I switched it for her, telling the goth I'd seen a fly in it.

Nobody ranted or cried today. The motorcycle guy bumped into Jeannette's chair and she didn't threaten to take out his lights. A mellow afternoon for my farewell visit.

How did you say goodbye to people who couldn't remember hello? Once I'd left, it would be as if I'd never come. I didn't even try to tell them I was leaving, just in case it upset them.

"I wish I'd bought them all presents," I told Cole as we waited for the bus.

"Your presence is the only present they require. Same as me. Come on Valentine's Day." He put his jester's hat back on. Taking anything seriously that came from under that hat was impossible.

"Maybe I will."

He grabbed my hand. "Don't say maybe. You've already given away his ring."

"It's gonna be so hard, Cole. His locker's across from mine. Sometimes he just makes me feel so good. Loved, you know?"

"Come to the home on Valentine's Day. Let me take you out after. You'll see, it will be worth it."

"I don't know." But I did know, really. Cole had made me want to break up with Donny since the moment I met him.

"You can't stay with him. He's not good enough for you. I mean maybe I'm not either, I get that. But he'll get you into all kinds of trouble."

He was right; I knew it. I should have told him right then and there that it was definitely off between Donny and me. I would be there for Cole on Valentine's Day. But I thought I had to tell Donny first, thought I owed him that much. What neither of us knew was just how much trouble Cole, himself, would get me into.

chapter twenty-one

"Your Honour, for the defence's next witness, we would like to call the defendant to the stand."

I get up, knees shaking, and walk wobbly to the witness box. Does the jury notice? Do they think I'm nervous because I've got something to hide?

"State your name for the record," my lawyer tells me quietly.

"Sonja Ehret."

"Do you wish to swear an oath or make an affirmation?"

I can't help checking out those twelve people now in charge of the next three years of my life as I choose to make the affirmation. Right now I don't believe in God. Maybe if Mom gets good news from the doctor on Thursday morning that will change. Are the jury members churchgoers? What do they think of me at this moment?

"Could you tell us in your own words what happened on February 14, when you visited Paradise Manor?"

"No."

The lady with the soya stain leans forward.

Heh, heh, the guy in the front coughs nervously.

"Are you refusing to answer your own attorney's

questions?" the judge asks.

"No, Your Honour. It's just I can tell you what I think happened on that day, but mostly I don't really know. I only know what I did and didn't do."

"All right." Michael McCann smiles at me. "Can you tell us your part in the events that took place that afternoon?"

I have to be absolutely truthful about every detail. I can't slip up or the jury may think I'm lying about the whole thing. That's why I said no that first time. I hope that buys me points for honesty with them.

"On Valentine's Day I was heading for Paradise Manor after school as I always did once a week for my volunteer credit. Only by this time I had finished my forty hours. That made me a regular visitor. Regular visitors don't have to follow all the student volunteer rules. I mean, I've never seen adult visitors be reminded to wash their hands and they can visit the residents alone in their rooms.

"To be honest, I wanted to drop off a few presents to the seniors I had worked closely with as a kind of goodbye. And I was going to meet Cole Demers to go out with him afterwards.

"That afternoon Donovan gave me a lift to the mall to pick up the presents. He was also going to drive me to the Manor afterwards, only we had an argument. I decided to take the bus. Because of that, I was about forty-five minutes later than usual. I don't know why Cole didn't wait. I mean, he was supposed to help out with the party, so he should have been there for at least another hour."

That's what I tell the courtroom but in my mind I replay the last time I saw Cole and the look on his face. What I find hard to live with is the reason he didn't stick around to see me.

The Forty-First Hour

I turned in my volunteer journal and thought I was well on the way to an A+. From then on I could do what I wanted, get the job at Salon Teo and visit the Manor whenever. Everything would be perfect, especially after I dumped Donny.

Whether or not Donovan had just found the pin on the floor didn't matter. Every smile or touch seemed like a lie to me now. If he told me I was beautiful, it just made me wonder what he wanted from me. When he smiled, I felt he was posing for a camera. Even his curls seemed artificial; I found myself wondering if he'd had his hair permed.

So I had the talk with him at school at lunch. We went for a walk around the football field and as we strolled, I started. "Donovan, we've been together almost eight months —"

"Best months of my life. When you're beside me, I feel like . . . I dunno . . . Superman. Nothing can bring me down." He didn't even stop walking to look at me. If anything, he moved quicker. Did he sense what was coming?

"Eight months is a really long time and we're young —"

He interrupted. "But it seems like no time at all. Now I understand how a guy can stay with one woman for life. I can see that with you, Sunny."

"No."

He slowed down. "Well, I know we're young. Especially you. And I'm not pressuring you —"

"No, we're not going to be together forever. Trust me on that one."

"I know you're ticked about the camera pin. But you're changing me. I'm becoming a better person. That's how much you mean to me."

"Donovan. I'm breaking up with you."

"No, no. You can't. You don't even know all I'm doing to change." He stopped and grabbed my wrist. "You have to give me another chance. Let me prove myself to you."

"We're finished, Donny. I'm sorry."

"No. No! Wait till Valentine's Day. You'll see. I'm going to do something for you that will change your mind about everything."

"I have to be at the Manor that day. I want to help with their party."

"Then I'll drive you. You know you never get there on time when you take the bus."

"Okay, fine." It wasn't though. Once you're done with a person, you really don't want to be around him and I shouldn't have accepted the lift. It gave him too much hope.

After school on Monday, he was right at my locker waiting. I tried to smile. "Do you think we could make a quick stop at the mall? I want to get a few little gifts for the residents."

"You have money?" he asked.

"Yes, I'm not asking you to pike anything."

"Sunny!" he held his chest as if I'd stabbed his heart. Again he rushed to open the car door. We passed the city bus and instinctively I looked up to see if I could find a jester's hat in the window. But the streets were dry and it was bright out, so Cole probably took his bike.

We got to the mall and I picked up some chocolate, one of those singing stuffed bears that sang "That's What Friends Are For" when you squeezed its paw, and some carnations. I couldn't afford the roses.

Back at the car, Donovan opened the trunk and got a long garment bag from it.

"What's that?" I asked.

He opened my car door. "Sit and you'll see."

I got in and he draped the bag across my knee. I couldn't open it. I wanted it to go away.

He ran to get in on the other side. "Go on. Look!" He grinned at me.

I unzipped the bag a few centimetres, just enough to see the shimmery blue fabric. "You didn't!" I gasped.

"My dad advanced me my first cheque. I'm working at the doughnut shop. I didn't get the pizza job."

"You have to take it back." I zipped the bag up again.

"No, no. I want to do this for you."

He wasn't making this any easier. "Donovan, I'm not going to the prom with you." My voice sounded loud to me. He had to have heard me, but was he registering any of it?

His eyes looked blank.

"I'm not going out with you any more. We're through. There's nothing you can do to change that."

He put his head down on the steering wheel then, not saying a word. This was a different Donny. Was he crying?

Oh my god! What could I do? I reached over to give him a bit of a back rub, to make him feel better. "There, there. It'll be all right." He wouldn't look up. I gave him a comforting hug. Not too long. Still, from the corner of my eye I saw movement.

I jumped back and saw a red bike. Cole? I waved, feeling a bit lighter and happier to see him.

His head turned but he didn't wave back. He didn't smile. He looked disappointed, sad even.

Oh my god, what had he seen? What was he thinking? I jumped out of the car, scrambling to collect the presents I had dropped.

"Cole!" I yelled and waved wildly. Way too far ahead. He didn't hear me. I had to catch up to him, to explain. That hug meant nothing! I ran to the bus stop. I heard Donovan's car tires squeal around the corner as he took off.

The bus took forever, circling the whole town. People got on and people got off at every single stop. Up the stairs, down. It made me crazy. I had to catch up to Cole and tell him I'd done it. I was free. We could see each other outside of Paradise Manor now.

Rush-hour traffic crawled, blocking every turn, slowing the bus into a four-wheeled turtle. It was turning into one of those nightmares: you know the kind where you try and try to get somewhere but somehow it's always just a little farther out of your reach. I began to think I would never get to Cole.

"Oh, great!" The police had blocked the street directly to the Manor. The bus had to take a detour.

"Looks like there's been an accident," a lady with shopping bags told the driver. "I hope nobody got hurt."

A siren warbled in that moment.

"Must have just happened," he answered back. "Here comes the ambulance."

I didn't know where the bus would go from there, so I stood up to ring the signal bell. Something made me turn to look back. A red light pulsed across my eyes. I squinted. *It isn't,* I told myself. *It couldn't be.*

chapter twenty-two

My lawyer jumps in with another question. "Maybe there is a detail you can clarify for the court. Why did Cole ride a bike that night if he meant to go out with you afterwards?"

I close my eyes for a second, open them and sigh. "As long as there was no ice on the road, he always rode his bike. Taking the bus takes twice as long, and that's if you're at the stop at just the right time. Besides the bus, if you don't have a licence you have to rely on parents or friends with cars. Cole just wanted to do his own thing."

"But you two were going to go out after."

"I don't know if he planned to leave his bike at the Manor and take a cab after. But I would have taken the bus or ridden on his bike with him if he'd asked." Whoops. Did I go too far? Riding two on a bike was illegal. Did that show I didn't mind breaking the law and so I would easily be able to help Helen Demers die?

"Sunny," Michael says gently, "did you know what had happened to Cole when you arrived at Paradise Manor?"

I shake my head. "But the bus I was on passed the accident. The ambulance arrived as we made the detour and I saw a crumpled bike at the side of the road. I'd hoped it wasn't

Cole's, but not that many people bike in February and it was red like his." Tears burn at the back of my eyes. My fists bunch. It's been a whole year since Cole rode away from Paradise Manor. How many times will I cry over that? I have to blink and that sends a tear sliding down my cheek. I don't wipe it away — I don't want to call attention to it.

"Did you continue with your regular volunteer activities?" Michael asks me.

"No, because it wasn't a regular volunteer hour anyway."

"Right." Michael nods. "This would have been your forty-first hour."

"Yes. But I had this awful feeling. When I stepped through the door of Paradise Manor, my head felt like it was floating off my body. Still, I followed all the rules, signing the book, washing my hands, keying in the lockup code. I passed out my gifts to the residents, but I didn't stop to chat with them. I couldn't.

"Only Jeannette was holding a bag of candies. She told me she'd taken them from Helen Demers's room. Cole never leaves those behind, so I thought maybe he'd just gone to the bathroom.

"I took them back from her and headed for Mrs. Demers's room. I saw some of the aides talking and the way one looked at me, I knew something was wrong.

"Still I wasn't sure what. I ran to Mrs. Demers's room, hoping Cole would have returned by now."

"But he hadn't," Michael says gently.

I shook my head. "No. So I sat down beside Mrs. Demers and I heard, we both heard, the receptionist, Katherine Filmore, tell someone that Cole had been hit by a car. Thrown. I couldn't move or do anything for a while."

Michael coaxes me on. "Do you feel Mrs. Demers

understood what was said about the accident?"

I shook my head. "I couldn't tell. Mrs. Demers just stared at me, not saying anything."

"But this would have been perfectly normal for her in her condition, correct?"

"Yes, but it did feel different. I reached out and touched her hand and she called me Cole and asked if I could give her a butterscotch."

"Would she normally have been able to speak in full sentences like that?" Michael McCann asked me.

"No, not for a month she hadn't. So I unwrapped one and put it in her mouth for her."

"Did she begin to choke?"

"No, she didn't. I didn't take the rest of the bag with me because it didn't belong to me. And honestly, Mrs. Demers couldn't walk anymore. She was in a wheelchair. There was no way she should have been able to reach the rest on the bureau where I left them.

"But at that moment I just couldn't stand being there any longer. I left her room and ran down the hall and out of the building. I know I didn't sign out or talk to anybody. But I couldn't deal with anything at that moment."

"To the best of your knowledge, you did not kill Mrs. Demers with that one candy, then?"

"I'm positive I didn't." What I don't tell them is that she motioned to me for another butterscotch. I waited for a second but she moaned and waved her hands. In a minute I thought she would start yelling the way Jeannette did when you didn't humour her. So I unwrapped a second candy slowly. I didn't want to give it to her. She hadn't even eaten the first one. I just wanted to play along with her, to comfort her. Just as the staff always did.

"No further questions."

"Mr. Dougal, do you wish to cross examine the witness?" the judge asks the buzzard.

"Yes, I do, Your Honour." He stands up and flicks at the back of his robe. His black feathers unfold behind him. He clears his throat. "Miss Ehret, you appear to be crying. Are you sad that a seventy-six-year-old woman died last year?"

"Objection!" Michael McCann calls.

"Overruled," the judge says. He turns to me. "You may answer the question."

That buzzard saw my one tear and he knows it isn't for Helen. *That sarcastic tone of his.* What should I answer? Should I be honest? I wipe both cheeks with my hands and take a breath. "Yes, I am sad."

"But you knew she was dying of Alzheimer's. That she couldn't walk or talk or even eat the things she liked anymore."

"Yes, I'm sad for all those things too."

"Aren't you really sad over Cole's accident?"

I nod. "Yes."

"Which are you sadder about?"

I shake my head and shrug my shoulders. "Cole was my friend and I lost him that day."

"Aren't you really just upset about having to stand and testify in front of all these people?"

"No . . . I mean yes. All of it. Honestly, I didn't even know I was crying."

The buzzard tilts his head in disbelief. "Do you always tell the truth?"

I stare into the buzzard's eyes for a few seconds and swallow hard to give the answer he doesn't expect. "No."

The lady in the front row pulls back likes she's been slapped.

"On February 14, when you knew Cole had been in a serious accident, did you really give Mrs. Demers only one candy?" His buzzard eyes brand me.

I answer quickly. "Yes." I never *gave* her another butterscotch. After I held the unwrapped Werther's in my hand for a moment, she kept up with the moaning, only louder. Then she reached over and, with her mouth to my hand, took the candy like a dog. Then she gestured for another. Mesmerized, I unwrapped it and she took it in the same way. I didn't have a clear idea of what she was doing but I had a feeling. I think she would have kept asking for more but I ran out.

"Do you expect the court to believe that this woman, who rarely spoke and couldn't walk, suddenly reached over and took two more candies, unwrapped them, and stuffed them down her own throat so that she would choke?"

"No. Yes. Maybe . . ." I begin to sputter now. This was so important for my mother, that I not be guilty.

"Didn't you, in fact, keep giving Mrs. Demers candy till she started coughing? Didn't you then quickly walk away, hoping she would die? Thereby helping your friend Cole out with a promise to his grandmother that you knew he couldn't keep?"

I feel my skin heat up. Had I heard her coughing? There was a rasping sound, not unlike what that juror is doing right now.

Heh, heh, heh!

Johann used to cough like that. It could have been anybody. Did I think it was Cole's grandmother? Doesn't matter, I didn't go back to check. "No!" My voice comes out whiny. I can't admit any of my true thoughts. It might spoil everything. I don't like the way everyone's staring at me.

"No further questions."

I know I haven't done well. I can see the chubby guy rubbing his forehead. That man in the front is coughing again.

I'd help you if you were choking, honest I would.

But I also know my lawyer has one more witness to call. Everything now depends on my mother. "Your Honour, I call Ursula Ehret to the stand."

My mother gets up and walks to the front. She's tall and long necked, graceful as a swan. Would that set her apart from the jury? What about that slight upper-crust Oxford accent?

She places her hand on the Bible and swears to tell the whole truth.

"How would you describe the way your daughter behaved at home?"

"Sonja has been a delight since the day she was born. She adored and looked up to her older brother. She was never disobedient to my husband or me. Never sloppy. She always kept her room tidy. She did her own laundry and helped with chores. Always respectful, no problem with drugs or skipping school." My mother lifts her hands and spreads them out like two birds flying away from her. "Never in trouble like some teenagers get into."

Is she forgetting our arguments over Donovan? Does she not remember when she was called in to Economart over the shoplifting incident? What about the report cards? She threw them to the table and huffed in disgust. "Too much time in front of the mirror." What about the arguments over coming to help at the condo office like dear old Wolfie?

Is my mother lying? I look into her tired blue eyes, tiny

wrinkles crowfooting from around them. The blue looks as though it has faded, is fading, along with my mother. What will the doctor say about her cancer on Thursday? Remarkably, in that moment she smiles at me, like there's a secret between us that she's going to keep.

"How would you say Sunny related to elderly people?"

"She loved them. When we first came to this country, my husband and I worked such long hours, so we brought my mother over to help us look after the children. It was my mother who nicknamed our Sonja 'Sunny' because she always brought smiles and joy to everyone around her. Especially my mother."

In German *Sonnenshein*. I hear the music and her voice in my head.

You are my sunshine, my only sunshine, you make me happy when skies are grey.

"How did she react to your mother's death? She died of cancer when Sunny was six, correct?"

"Yes. She didn't understand. Maybe we should not have taken her to the funeral. She seemed lost and very sad. She drew pictures of her Omi leaving her in a plane and on a boat."

The music and singing stops.

"Two summers ago, you fought a battle with cancer. How did this affect Sunny?"

"We didn't realize so much at the time . . . but she pulled away. She didn't come to our family's business office anymore. She started seeing this boy . . ."

"Donovan Petrocelli?"

"Correct. And we forbade her to see him because he got into trouble."

"Did she listen?"

"No. But my husband and I let it go. We were busy with the hospital appointments . . . and the business. We didn't ask her too much so she didn't have to lie. We knew she was a smart girl and would figure it out for herself."

"What about the hair colouring? The pink streaks in her hair."

My mother smiles at me again. "That's when I knew my Sunny was coming back to me."

"Could you explain?"

"As I was going through treatments for breast cancer, Sunny did not want to be around me. I thought she was angry with me for becoming sick. But she could not talk about it. When she put the pink streaks in her hair, I didn't ask. I didn't have the strength to discuss and argue. But then her friend Alexis explained."

"What did she say to you?"

"That Sunny thought I was leaving her just like her grandmother. That Alexis tried to get her to do the Run for the Cure but she couldn't do it. Instead she dyed her hair pink at the front almost like the ribbons they give out."

The lady with the soya sauce down her front turns slightly to look at me. She smiles.

Anybody can spill sauce, I think.

"What about Sunny's volunteer work at the home?"

"My husband and I thought it was the best thing for her. We weren't sure when Sunny attended the funerals at the home. But then we could see that maybe it even helped her. She realized that people are . . ." my mother hesitates and makes a quick eye contact with me again, "mortal, through no fault of their own. They do not die to leave someone."

"Mrs. Ehret, do you believe she might have wanted to aid

in a mercy killing or suicide last February 14?"

"Absolutely not. I feel she was very upset by the accident. That she was in shock and could not react and behave normally."

"Do you think she walked away as Helen Demers began choking to death?"

"No, no, no." My mother rubs at her eyes and when she looks up again, they are tear filled. "It doesn't matter how upset she was, she would not leave this woman to die."

"Thank you. No further questions."

"Mr. Dougal, do you have questions for the witness?"

"No . . . wait. Yes, Your Honour." The buzzard flies up and faces my mother.

I sit back, knowing there is nothing he can say to rattle or trip her up in any way.

"Mrs. Ehret, we can tell that you love your daughter and that you are proud of her."

My mother smiles and nods.

"Would you say that you would do anything in your power to protect her?"

"Yes, yes but . . ."

"No further questions."

The lady in the sweatsuit frowns and looks as upset as I feel that the buzzard cut Mom off. My mother would lie for me, that's how it sounds. How can Michael McCann ever get the jury to acquit me if they think even my mother lies? I sit waiting for the judge to call it a day but then, surprisingly, my lawyer stands up again.

"Your Honour, we would like to ask the court's indulgence. We want to call one last witness up. We were uncertain whether he would be physically capable of testifying but it now appears he can. We call Cole Demers to the stand, please."

Mrs. Johnson gasps. A surprise witness. For once we both feel the same about something: shocked. There's some murmuring between the reporter and Mrs. Demers.

The judge calls for order. "Members of the court are reminded that their reactions can influence the jury and therefore should be reserved for outside this room. Otherwise, they could be used as a grounds for mistrial."

Meanwhile, a tall, pale boy I hardly recognize makes his way slowly to the front. Cole looks heavier than when I last saw him and he drags his left foot slightly. When he finally sits down in the witness box and faces me, I see a zipper-like scar stretching from the corner of his left eye to his upper lip.

I swallow hard, but then he smiles. The smile doesn't make it up to his eyes, but they take me in.

I smile back. His hair doesn't stand up anymore at the top but it's grown really long and shaggy. I could so fix that for him.

Cole doesn't stutter when he swears on the Bible but there are gaps in his speech.

"Thank you for coming today," my lawyer tells him. "The court understands that you are still recovering from your accident last year. For the record, have you spoken to the defendant, Sonja Ehret, since then?"

"No." Cole furrows his brow. "Conditions for her bail are . . . no contact."

He was in a coma for two months after the accident, but I couldn't visit him. I heard from Alexis when he opened his eyes, but I wasn't allowed to send him a note. I found out about him speaking a month later, but I couldn't call. There was no way to tell him how sorry I was about everything. I hadn't heard he could walk.

My lawyer didn't know whether he would call Cole to the stand or not. He wasn't certain which way his condition might swing the jurors.

Michael must feel desperate.

He doesn't sound it, though. He leans on the podium and speaks in a casual tone. "Can you tell us what your relationship was with Sunny?"

"We were . . . friends."

"Boyfriend-girlfriend friends?" Michael smiles.

"I'd hoped." He smiles back and that gives the jury members permission to titter and grin.

The judge doesn't say anything about the reactions this time.

Michael continues. "About your grandmother's pink streaks, could you tell the court how they came about?"

"Sure. It was . . . Grandma's birthday present. Sunny did them for her."

"Did she steal money from your grandmother's drawer to buy the dye?"

"No! I gave her the mo. . .ney. I asked her to streak Grandma's hair . . . because she liked Sunny's."

"So you didn't go along with her idea. It was your decision to colour the hair."

"Yes. My idea."

I watch for the jury's reaction. The guy with the crooked glasses nods. I think he may be shifting to my side.

My lawyer straightens and gestures to Cole with an open palm. "I know how difficult this is for you, but could you tell the jury how your grandmother felt about her Alzheimer's?"

"Yes." Cole pauses a longer while.

The bearded juror with the piercings shifts in his chair.

The woman formerly of the sweatsuit leans forward. Yes he can, or yes he will, everyone must be wondering from the long delay.

Finally Cole speaks again. "She asked me to help her . . . die."

Michael nods. "And did you agree?"

"Yes."

Someone on the jury gasps.

"Did you tell Sunny about your grandmother's request?"

"Yes."

"Do you remember what she said?"

"I think . . . I think she told me to forget about it. Not to feel . . . bad. It wasn't a reasonable request."

"Did you give your grandmother candy at the end of every visit?"

"Yes. Other times, too. She liked . . . sweets."

"You left Paradise Manor before the Valentine's party. Why?"

Cole shuts his eyes for a moment. "I was . . . angry. I thought Sunny was bringing Donovan . . . I couldn't stay."

I cover my face. If I had just told Donovan he couldn't drive me that day, none of this would have happened.

"Was it Sunny's fault that you had your accident that day?"

Cole shakes his head. "No." His face turns red, he looks too upset to continue.

Michael watches him and waits patiently.

Cole starts again. "I rode a bike in February. I didn't wear a helmet. I was . . . stupid."

"Do you think Sunny gave your grandmother candies till she choked and then just walked away?"

"No." He shakes his head. "Never."

"Thank you. No further questions."

The judge asks the Crown whether he has any questions. I can see the buzzard think for a moment.

"Yes, Your Honour. I do." He stands and turns towards the witness box. "Mr. Demers, you have suffered through severe brain trauma, is that correct?"

"Yes."

"And you said just now that you think Sonja Ehret told you to forget your grandmother's request. Is that right?"

"Yes."

"Is it not true that memory lapses are a symptom of brain trauma?"

Someone groans in the jury.

"I'm sure . . . she told me not to help Grandma. Just not sure about the wording."

"Answer the question Mr. Demers," the buzzard snaps. "Are memory lapses symptoms of your condition or not?"

"Sometimes."

"No further questions."

I stare at Cole and wish for the millionth time that I could just talk to him.

He returns my stare. Suddenly he winks and that makes me feel a whole lot better. Then he gets up and slowly limps out of the courtroom.

I want to jump up and chase after him, but I know I can't.

The judge clears his throat as he looks at his watch. "The time is now three p.m. We shall adjourn till tomorrow for the final summations."

We do the whole standing-up routine for the judge who leaves by his side entrance. Then my parents and I walk out the front.

"Don't worry. Everything went well," Michael tells me, grabbing my hand and squeezing it. "Tomorrow it will be my turn. Go home and try to forget about the trial. Have a nice family evening."

Mom nods and Dad agrees out loud as we slip our coats on. The surrounding cement walls are heavy and claustrophobic, and I feel as though everyone is looking at me. Quickly, I lead the way down a couple of flights of stairs and through a double set of doors. Finally, I take a deep breath outside. It's February. A warm one like last year when it happened, but still grey and bleak.

On the way to the car, Mom calls Wolfie on her cell. She tells him about how today went for us and asks him if there are things that need their attention at the office. "Okay, then we will come."

A nice family evening performing condo management duties.

"Wait, Mom!" I catch her arm before she gets into the car.

She hesitates, one hand still on the door.

"Did you mean what you said on the stand back there?"

"Sunny! Of course. Every word."

"But it wasn't all true. I was trouble for you and Dad."

"You are our daughter, no trouble to us."

My mother has a different way of speaking and I want so badly to understand.

"What if I am guilty?"

She sighs. "What is guilty?" She reaches out and touches the left side of my chest with one hand. "Your heart is good. I know this. Your father and your brother know this, too." She looks into my eyes and grabs my forearms "When I am old, you will dye some of my hair pink too, yes?"

"Sure Mom."

"You are never guilty."

I put my arms around her. She's thin and breakable. It does too matter what the stupid people decide. Her eyes and smile will fade. Her bones will crumble, she'll turn to dust and blow away. I want to say more to her, to be the kid I used to be when I was little, all adoring.

But I let her go and we all get into the car.

When we get to the office, Wolfie tells me that Alexis called. "She said Mr. Brooks is bringing the whole class tomorrow."

"Don't look that way," my father says. "Your friends wish to support you."

"Yeah, but it's not like a basketball game where they can cheer."

He tilts his head. "Nevertheless, it's nice."

"No homework either for the weekend," Wolfie tells me.

"Now that's nice."

"I want to come too," my brother suddenly announces.

Dad glances at Mom.

"It should be the last day." She answers his unspoken question. "We can close the office. I will have news from the doctor tomorrow morning, too."

Discussion over, we settle into our usual routine. I open the mail, stamp it, circle amounts, and pass it to Mom. Dad calls a few contractors. This is what our family does together, office work. I smile, looking at my mother. She believes in me.

The routine is comforting but when our pizza comes it's hard to eat. Did I say the right things? What could I have done differently? The jury knows I lie sometimes. I admitted it myself. Will that be enough to convict me?

Before bed, my mother and I sip a cup of herbal tea that's supposed to make you sleep. My mother hugs me for a long time. She loves me, likes me too, no matter what. I think knowing that helps me sleep best of all.

chapter twenty-three

The next day Mom is late from her doctor's appointment. As I check the door of the courtroom, I try to make a bargain with a God I don't even believe in. *Trade you my not guilty verdict for a no cancer diagnosis.* If Mom is cancer free it won't matter if I have to go away for a little while. I watch my classmates drift in. Mr. Brooks finds a seat. Donovan next and Alexis, then Gillian Halliday from the residence. Where is Mom? Has she already been admitted to hospital?

The judge calls for order several times and threatens to clear the room before everyone finally settles down. Then he looks toward my lawyer.

"Attorney for the defence?" the judge says. Michael McCann stands up.

"Members of the jury, Your Honour, Crown Counsel, all teenagers do not lie, steal, or break the law. Some of them like seniors, some of them enjoy volunteering with old people. Some of them respect their parents and teachers, do their homework and chores. We've heard that Sonja is one of those kinds of young people.

"We've also heard how difficult the death of her own grandmother was to her. How hard she took the news of her mother's bout with cancer. This is a young person who values life in both the young and the old.

"On February 14 of last year, Sonja Ehret walked into Mrs. Demers's room. The two overheard the news of Cole's accident. Whether Mrs. Demers understood or not, she did something unusual. She requested a candy. On a normal day she couldn't speak anymore. Perhaps she was having one of her 'good days.' Sonja unwrapped it and gave it to her. Then, upset as she was over Cole, she left.

"Witnesses for the Crown testify that Sonja Ehret breaks rules. She didn't break a rule that day entering the room alone. She was no longer there as a student volunteer.

"Did she break a rule giving Helen Demers a candy? Perhaps. But Cole had been giving Helen candies every visit. Should she be expected to think that it could cause fatal harm to Helen? I don't believe so.

"What happened then? There is a possibility that in this better state that Mrs. Demers was in, this small temporary reprise from her condition, she could have reached over, unwrapped another two candies, and popped them in her mouth.

"Or perhaps, as Sunny suggested, one of the other patients came in and helped her ingest more candy.

"The good state ended and she began to choke. If the Crown could prove that Sonja heard this choking and did not return to assist her or call someone else, this would be an unlawful act. Unfortunately, no one noticed in time to help Mrs. Demers. We've already heard how busy Paradise Manor could get sometimes.

"Even if you believe that the afternoon might have played out the way the Crown has suggested, you must find Sonja

213

Ehret not guilty. If you think Sunny probably or likely fed Mrs. Demers candy till she choked and then denied her any assistance, you must still find Sunny not guilty. As the judge told you in his instructions at the beginning of the trial, 'maybe,' 'likely,' even 'probably' is not good enough. Sunny is innocent unless the Crown Counsel has convinced you *beyond any reasonable doubt* that she committed this crime. One thing that is certain to me, and it should be evident to the court, is that Sonja Ehret did not kill Helen Demers. Alzheimer's disease killed Helen Demers. And you cannot hold anyone accountable for this unfortunate disease. Thank you."

I feel a hand on my shoulder and turn to see Mom has arrived. She smiles and whispers in my ear. "Everything is good."

A smile cracks my face open wide and I breathe out a long sigh as I squeeze her hand on my shoulder. Nothing else will matter.

"Will the Crown Counsel present his summation now," the judge commands.

The buzzard's eyes blink in a near twitch. He looks towards me and back to the judge. Finally he stands up, clears his throat, and begins.

"In this country we do not believe in euthanasia, nor do we believe that patients can choose to end their own lives. This is in our law.

"We have this law so that the weak and the helpless and, yes, the feebleminded, are protected.

"We have heard from several witnesses that Sonja Ehret broke regulations when it suited her. When Sonja came that extra day, she told us that the regular rules did not apply.

"Yes, Sonja Ehret liked old people. She wanted them to

have choices. When Helen Demers wanted pink hair, Sonja gave her pink hair. She wanted sweets, Cole and Sonja gave them to her.

"She asked for death and her grandson Cole couldn't give it to her because he obeyed rules. But Sonja Ehret did not.

"She claims she only gave Helen Demers a single butterscotch but she also admitted that she doesn't always tell the truth. She lied about the sewer explosion, she lied to sneak around with a forbidden boyfriend. Members of the jury, she's lying about that single candy.

"The coroner's report states clearly that three candies were lodged in Helen Demers's throat. It also confirms the time of death to be five-forty. Sonja left at five-thirty. Beyond any reasonable doubt, she was the last person to see Helen Demers alive.

"On February 14. Cole's near-fatal accident convinced her that Helen Demers should die. We know Sonja took first-aid courses and understood how to perform the Heimlich manoeuvre. Sonja gave Mrs. Demers candies until she choked, then refused assistance to her. She didn't call anyone to help Helen Demers. Sonja walked away. The candy caused the choking, but Sonja denying her medical assistance was an unlawful act, one that a reasonable person could foresee causing serious harm.

"Yes, Sonja liked old people and bought them things and wanted only to please them. This was not a murder for money or personal gain. This was a misguided effort to help a senior.

"But it is manslaughter nonetheless. And misguided as she was, she is accountable. Members of the jury, it is your duty to see that she is held accountable. I ask you to find her guilty."

Those twelve people all stare at me now, no smiles from any of them. Do they think they can see the truth in my eyes? I thought that if my mother's ultrasound was clear, I wouldn't care about all this. But now I find I still do. One of the bearded twins scratches at his chin. *Heh, heh,* the man in the front coughs.

I study the jury, too, and can't see through their expressions any more than they see through mine. It's been a year since it all happened. I don't think I can listen to one more question or statement about that Valentine's Day. Mom is okay, that's all that matters. But the judge speaks just as Michael McCann warned me he would. He has to make his formal charge to the jury.

First he talks about their duties and how they have to decide based upon all the facts presented to them — not anything they've heard in the media, not public opinion or their own sympathies, prejudices, or fears. They don't have to worry about punishment, they just need to discuss, listen, and decide the case for themselves. *Blah, blah, blah.* On and on he talks about witnesses, exhibits. He reviews the testimonies. I want to explode, he's crammed so much law into it. Finally, it all seems to boil down to this: I gave her candies until she began choking and then walked away. I withheld medical assistance. If that's what all twelve of them believe beyond a reasonable doubt, they should find me guilty.

"The jury will now retire to make its deliberations."

"All rise," the court clerk commands. The twelve members shuffle out.

"What do we do now?" I ask Michael.

"We wait."

"How long?" I ask.

216

"It depends how fast they make up their minds and whether they all agree on the verdict. Why don't you go to the cafeteria and I will call you."

"Can we go outside somewhere instead?" I plead. "Everyone else will be in the cafeteria."

"Sure," Michael answers.

My father nods. Once outdoors, there's a parking lot but no sidewalk and no decent mall nearby. No place for us to go.

Some kids from my class are outside smoking. I don't wave.

"We can cross the street and walk for a bit over there." My mother points to a strip mall.

My father grabs our hands. He wants to keep us safe from the cars, from the dangerous outside world. He grips too tightly because he just can't save us from that inside world behind us. Wolfie grabs on to my other hand. This is all I need. I feel safe.

At the little strip, there's a Greek diner, a convenience store, a pharmacy, and a doughnut shop. No one wants a coffee or doughnuts so my father picks up a wild-cherry gum pack from the convenience store. He opens the package, offering them around outside. I take one. My mouth is so dry. I chew, but then it's too sweet. Wolfie grabs two.

I see my mother huddling from cold as she pulls out a single stick for herself. We should have stayed inside the court building. The weather is too much for her.

"Mom?" Purple shadows her eyes, she couldn't have slept. We could still lose her; a doctor's okay this morning is not a guarantee. I want to say something to her what I couldn't say for a long time. It's hard for me so I try in German first. "*Ich liebe dich.*" She looks at me, startled. I reach out and hug her gently. "I love you, Mom."

Dad's cell phone goes off then. We break apart. "It's too soon," he says. "How can they have decided so quickly?" He sounds anxious, as though an early decision will not be the one we hope for. "Hello. Yes, yes." He snaps the phone shut. "It's time. We have to go back."

We return to the court with the others. I take my special seat with my parents and brother in the row behind me. There is a buzz of people as the court fills again.

The judge looks up at the jury. Finally, he says: "Have you agreed upon a verdict?"

Heh, heh, heh. The nervous cougher stands. "We have, Your Honour." He coughs again. "We find the defendant . . . not guilty."

Behind me kids leap up and cheer. I step down from my box into the aisle where Mom jumps up to join me. We hug and my father hugs around us. Wolfie joins our circle. I'm as overjoyed that the whole thing is over as I am about the verdict.

Michael McCann shakes my hand and wishes me good luck.

"Thank you so much." I hug him when we finish hand shaking. When I look up I see Mr. Brooks. We hug too.

"Sunny, I always knew you were innocent. I adjusted your marks for last year. You'll have an A+ on the journal and a B+ in English. You deserve it for all that you've been through."

"Thanks, Mr. Brooks."

I hug Alexis and high five with Chris and Josh. Some of my classmates pat my back.

Donovan looks at me but I can't touch him. "Shoulda never happened, Babe."

I nod. There is a reporter and the flash of a camera. My

father tells me he's okayed the shot so everyone everywhere will know that I'm innocent.

When the brightness ends, I think I see Cole's face. I feel a sharp pang in my chest. But when my eyes focus more clearly I can see that the face is an older, more wrinkled version and it belongs to his mother. No way would she have let Cole attend.

"Mrs. Demers!" I rush towards her and she turns away. "Don't go yet!"

She hesitates for a second, but then keeps walking.

It's that small hesitation that gives me hope. I want to grab her shoulders and make her listen to me. But my mother catches up to me and drapes one arm over my shoulder. "She is very sad right now. It is not your fault."

Mrs. Demers needs time, I get that. My mother thinks it's not my fault and Cole doesn't blame me either. He said so in his testimony. But it's the wink and smile I remember most. Maybe I won't be able to make things right with his mother, but I know I can help him. Help him with his physio, with his speech, whatever.

Everyone always said how good I was with old people. That's because I was patient. And my grandmother didn't nick-name me Sunny for nothing. I will bring sunshine into Cole's life again. If she sees her son growing stronger, won't Mrs. Demers be happy again too?

I just have to be patient.

The End

acknowledgements

A huge thank you to Brendan Neil, a criminal trial lawyer who often defends young people. Brendan guided me right from the premise of the story, through the trial process (I sat in on a couple of his trials), to the final verdict, suggesting scenarios and wording changes along the way. The condensing and other liberties taken with the Canadian justice system were purely for the sake of the story and all of my own.

Thank you also to test teen reader Ola Lukawski and to many other writers who read this story: Gisela Sherman, Lynda Simmons, Jennifer Filipowicz, Rory D'eon, and Jim Bennett, to name a few.

While the emotional pain of loss due to Alzheimer's disease are true to my own experience, the names, characters, places, and incidents were produced entirely from my imagination.

about the author

When Sylvia McNicoll was born (in Ajax, Ontario), her mother contemplated naming her Sonja or Sunshine. The family later moved to Montreal, Quebec, where Sylvia graduated from Concordia University. Her writing career began when she returned to Ontario with her husband and three children. She has written twenty-seven books for young people and has won the Silver Birch Award and the Manitoba Young Reader's Choice Award.

Sylvia enjoys long bike rides but always wears a helmet and never rides in the winter.